SHUTTERED REALITY

JASON ROBERTS SAGA - BOOK 1

SHUTTERED REALITY

EF CUSSINS

Library of Congress Control Number: 2024910384
Paperback ISBN: 979-8-9907532-0-4
Digital Book ISBN: 979-8-9907532-1-1

For my Family

GOOD INTENTIONS - BAD RESULTS

BAD INTENTIONS - GOOD RESULTS

EF CUSSINS

TO GERMANY

Few opportunities exist for an eighteen-year-old to graduate high school with a 2.5 grade point average and explore the world. The day I visited my local Army recruiter, he told me I could see the world and turn my hobby into a paying profession. I signed up right away.

Little did I realize over the years the photographs I took would either get me into trouble or save my butt. Some of them even changed the course of governments.

Let me start my story in the summer of 1966. I graduated from high school and left Boise, Idaho for boot camp at Fort Ord, California. While there, I realized I had no desire to kill other human beings. The only shooting I wanted to do was with a camera.

At the end of boot camp, the Army gave me the assignment of Eleven Baker (the Army's destination for Field Infantry). Because of my high scores, I convinced the Army to send me to Fort Meade in Maryland for twelve weeks of specialized training.

I spent the next twelve weeks at Fort Meade. The advanced training, for me, was more fun and work. I could tell several of my classmates were jealous because I got the highest scores. Finally, I achieved the official destination of Twenty-five Victor, (photographer and documentation).

They offered me the opportunity to stick around and become an assistant instructor. I turned it down for my choice of a duty station. I wanted to see the world. So, I chose Germany.

In my mind, I would be far away from the flying bullets of Vietnam and see some really neat places.

Upon arrival in Germany, I was assigned to a special Army Intelligence unit. I spent most of my time taking pictures over the Berlin Wall into the Soviet Sector. I was supplied with the latest and greatest specialized cameras with a powerful telephoto lens.

One time, I took a series of photos of a Russian officer in a hotel room. I could see it from the American side of the Berlin Wall. I caught him getting out of the shower. His towel fell to the floor. I snapped several pictures of his ass. That was not the embarrassing part. The printed photograph revealed a heart-shaped tattoo on his right butt cheek. Inside the heart was a woman's name.

Everybody got a laugh at the picture. We made sure that the photograph got used to blackmail that officer. The CIA loved me for getting that picture along with others I sent them.

LOVED GERMANY

In school, we were told about the destruction of Germany at the end of World War II. By 1967, many buildings and streets were rebuilt. A lot of the older shops and streets still existed. I enjoyed walking through cities in Germany where I could experience the old-world charm. I enjoyed walking on cobblestone streets and visiting the little mom-and-pop shops.

Like any talented photographer, I kept my Minolta camera around my neck. I was ready to snap a photograph of whatever caught my eye. Over my shoulder hung my camera bag. It housed a telephoto lens and extra rolls of film. On a one or two-day trip, I would fill three or four rolls from photos I had taken.

A couple weeks before the Christmas of 1967, I took leave in Hamburg. I spotted an older gentleman with a much younger woman. He looked familiar. So, I followed the couple from across the street. I watch them go in and out of the various stores. In my mind, I labeled them as May-December lovers.

Her beautiful blond hair flowed out from a large white fur hat that matched the fur coat. The seams in her coat appeared to have been sown with gold-colored thread. She carried a tiny black purse, a belt, and boots that matched. The boots had heels elevating her to almost the same height as her gentleman friend.

I had trouble placing where I had seen him before. Just as I raised my camera to take their pictures, I heard from behind me, "Corporal Roberts! What are you doing spying on the General?"

I turned to see standing not six feet from me, my staff sergeant. "No, sir!" Then I realized who I stood across the street from us. I had to say something to my sergeant. "Is that gentleman across the street the General? I know he looks familiar, but couldn't place him."

"That gentleman is General William Moorehead III, our commanding general."

My short time in the Army taught me to look at an officer's collar for rank and only look him in the eyes when being addressed. General Moorehead that day wore civilian clothes, and he didn't have his usual military escorts, either. I just saw the couple across the street were an older gentleman and a beautiful blond. Nothing about their behavior spoke military.

The sergeant gave me a quick piece of advice. "You better move along. If the General catches you stalking him, you can end up in the stockade or worse."

"Yes, sir, thank you for warning me, sir."

The sergeant took a few steps away from me when he stopped and turned toward me. "Walk with me, Corporal. I know a place that serves the best beer and food in Hamburg."

After lunch and a pitcher of beer, the sergeant reminded me about the protocol for taking pictures of superior officers. He even allowed me to take a few of him to send back to his family.

As the sergeant walked away. My thoughts went back to the General and the blond, whom I believed to be Mrs. Moorehead. I envied the General for having such a beautiful wife. Like any good soldier, I came up with a plan on how I could make points with my general. It would speed me up to an early promotion.

I DIDN'T KNOW

Later that day, in another part of the town, I came across the General and his lady friend again. In my mind, I pictured how the General and his wife would love a romantic photograph of them while Christmas shopping. I knew he would be bubbling over with pride. Any man in his late fifties who was lucky enough to have a trophy wife like her would want a perfect photograph of them together on his desk.

Snow-adorned windowsills flawlessly made the perfect backdrop. The late afternoon sun cast shadows and highlighted the couple's faces. I attached the telephoto lens to my camera. I knew that taking the right photo at the right moment would ensure me an early promotion. The thought entered my mind: if I entered their photo in the New York Times' annual photo contest, I would win.

Looking through my camera and the telephoto lens, I snapped several shots while they held hands with their fingers intertwined. Then I took this one shot when she whispered something in his ear and he smiled.

A dark thought tried to ruin the moment. In my mind, I heard my sergeant's voice, "Taking a picture of the General without him knowing about it could end you up in the stockade." It didn't take long before I could push those words out of my mind. All I could think about was how pleased the General and his wife would be when they saw the photo I took in a beautiful frame. What loving couple would not like a beautiful photograph of them?

The lovely couple were going in and out of all the really expensive-looking shops. Every time they came out of a shop, the General added another shopping bag with the store's logo.

Since I had about two weeks before Christmas, I took my time sorting through all the photos. Finally, I picked out the one with the best of the General and his wife. I enlarged it up to an eight by ten and used a coloring method with oil paints to make their faces stand out, then I put it in the best frame I could find and wrapped it in traditional Christmas paper.

A buddy from my unit with super nice handwriting made the tag for me. The tag read 'To General Moorehead and wife, From Corporal Jason Roberts'. I paid a soldier from the base mail service to hand deliver it to the General's residence.

Mrs. Moorehead didn't wait until Christmas to open their present. When she saw the photograph in the frame, she let out a scream the neighbors heard. I can only imagine the anger and hurt feeling she felt by seeing a photograph of her husband kissing some strange blond.

Later that day, when General Moorehead arrived at home he found his wife had thrown his clothes onto their snow-covered yard. After throwing out his clothes, she picked up the phone and called every officer's wife in all of West Germany. By the next morning, word had crossed over the Iron Curtain. KGB officers in Moscow were laughing about what I had done. I am sure General Moorehead had received a call or two from the Pentagon about his extramarital affair.

I woke up with MPs standing at the foot of my bunk with

orders to be escorted to General Moorehead III's office. There I stood between the two in handcuffs. I had trouble making out what he said because he spent so much of the time screaming at me. His face kept changing shades of red and purple. I thought he would have a heart attack or burst a blood vessel.

When the General finally calmed down. He told the MPs, "I want you to put him in the stockade and throw away the key." He stopped, thought for a moment, then said, "Better yet, take the bastard out and shoot him."

That morning, I was so thankful they didn't obey that order.

BACK TO THE STATES

From the perspective of a nineteen-year-old, all I did was press the shutter button on my camera. I just happened to have my camera pointing at a loving couple. Not even my sergeant hinted at the woman not being the General's wife. If he knew, he should have said something to me.

The MPs booked me into the stockade for stalking and attempting to blackmail General Moorehead. Over the next three days, all I could think about was my future in the Army and the looming possibility of my life being over. On the morning of the fourth day, the same two Army MPs appeared outside my cell. They escorted me to a nearby airfield and placed me on waiting transport to Fort Polk, Louisiana. During the entire trip, I sat between two other MPs handcuffed and shackled the entire distance.

The MPs told me the General's wife had flown back to the States with plans to divorce him. They heard a rumor General Moorehead would have a star taken away for conduct unbecoming an officer. They even teased me about being stationed somewhere unpleasant without a camera.

Throughout the whole time in the stockade and even when I got back to the States, I tried to explain my position. When I told my side of the story, some would snicker, others would laugh aloud. They all agreed sending that photograph had ended my career in the Army.

I had clearly violated regulations by taking a photograph of the General without his permission. I had support from the enlisted men. They thought any officer caught cheating on his wife. He deserved such embarrassment and demotion.

I received a suggestion to send copies of the photograph and the others I had taken to the local newspaper in the General's hometown. I quickly dismissed the idea. Fortunately, at the same time, I sent the General his photograph, I sent the negatives to my parents to put in storage with the rest of my stuff.

Upon my arrival at Fort Polk in Louisiana, the MPs took the shackles and handcuffs off before leaving the plane. I went straight from the plane to the commanding officer of the Fort. He informed me he had received orders for me to start Advance Combat Training. The current class has passed the halfway point. I had to wait for the next class to start. While waiting, I would be peeling potatoes in the morning and cleaning latrines in the evenings.

Among the enlisted men, I became sort of a hero. They loved the idea of me sticking it to a high-ranking officer. Some told me I should sell my story to a big newspaper like the New York Times. They said I could make lots of money. To be honest, I just wanted not to end up in Leavenworth for the rest of my life or dead.

After four days at Fort Polk, I got shipped off to Fort Bragg where another advanced combat training class would start on the following Monday. I just made it through those four weeks of hell.

Usually, upon completing the Advance Combat course, a soldier would get a week or more of leave before getting shipped off to their next assignment. Not me. It seemed no matter what I said or did; the Army intended to punish me by sending me directly to the last place I wanted to go; South Vietnam.

HELLO VIETNAM

In the Spring of 1968, a Pan American Boeing 747 touched down at the Tan Son Nhut Air Force Base in South Vietnam. It taxied to a waiting group of trucks and soldiers. Upon the flight attendant opening the front side door, in rushed a putrid green cloud mixed with hot, thick, humid air. I felt so nauseated, that I came close to splattering the seat in front of me.

I found out later the stench came from the place where they burned trash and human waste. Some officer must have come up with the sick idea of having new recruits offload downwind of where they burned sewage. What a way to get us ready for all the shit we were about to experience.

In a few hours, the plane we arrived on would refuel and with battle-warned soldiers and several body bags be heading back to the States.

When my boots touched the ground, I looked up to see this Army Captain heading toward me. His uniform had all the sharp creases in his shirt aligned with the sharp creases in his pants. On his head, a new Army cap. What amazed me most about the man, he didn't show one sign of sweat. His hat and jacket exceeded Army regulations. I couldn't understand how he could be so picture-perfect considering the heat and humidity. Not one sign of sweat appeared anywhere on him.

"Are you Corporal Jason Roberts?" he asked.

I stood up straight and gave him a perfect salute. "Yes, sir, Corporal Jason Roberts, Combat photographer reporting for duty, sir."

"I am Captain Reginald Phillips. I am under orders to escort you to the General. He wants to see you as soon as you arrive."

My mind raced with one big question: Why would a general want to see me as soon as I landed? Could General Moorehead have sent word to have me punished even more? I heard Moorehead had been assigned to some Army base in the Midwest. So, I was told.

Captain Phillips pointed to a nearby jeep. "Get in the back. I'll take you to him."

I chucked my duffel bag in the back and kept my camera case firmly attached to my shoulder. I jumped in behind the captain and his driver. Regardless, as much as I wanted to, I didn't ask questions. I had no clue what was in store for me. On that day, all I wanted to do was finish my tour of duty and get back to Idaho.

Through everything I had been through, that camera case and its contents were my security blanket. In my camera case, were my toys that gave me security and pleasure by using them. My favorite camera was a Minolta SR-2 with a telephoto and a wide-angle lens. Not a cheap camera, but it gave some of the best pictures I have ever taken. The telephoto lens allowed me to take sharp pictures from a safe distance. I also had a Yashica Electro 35. An inexpensive camera with a fast shutter speed enabled me to take action shots when in a combat situation. The Yashica being light and easy to use made for a perfect camera in a combat zone. Besides, if I lost the Yashica or it got damaged, it would not be as big a loss. If I lost that Minolta, I would cry.

Between basic training and the Advance Combat Course, they drummed into me the idea of killing the enemies of the United States. At that point in my life, I could not imagine watching the life force leave another human being.

FACING THE GENERAL

The captain's driver wasn't much older than me. His wavy blond hair was a little longer than regulation. On his shoulder were the stripes of a first sergeant. The captain and his driver's contradiction foreshadowed other contradictions, in a country filled with contradictions.

The sergeant drove us to the north end of the runway, where we came upon two rows of Quonset huts. Who would have thought something made for the Navy in World War II would be so popular? Built in a 16-by-36-foot structure framed with steel members having an 8-foot height. It looked more like half of a corrugated galvanized steel cylinder, cut lengthwise. These buildings served as shelters for soldiers and supplies. The fact they required minimal maintenance made them so popular.

The sergeant parked the Jeep next to the Quonset hut closest to the perimeter fence.

That hut looked like someone had used it for target practice from all the bullet holes. I wondered why the General would want to meet me here.

"Hop out soldier, the General is waiting for you inside," the captain ordered.

I crept through the door to see the back of an older gentleman wearing an Army olive green uniform. He looked busy inspecting the labels on the wooden crates. The screen door slammed closed behind me. He turned and gave me an evil stare.

In the Army, one gets trained to look at the collar of an officer. The insignia on the collar told me about the wearer's rank and how I should respond. This soldier had a signal star sown in black thread. The star told me I stood in the presence of a Brigadier General. I sprang to attention and raised my right hand above my brow.

"Corporal Jason Roberts reporting as ordered, sir."

"Welcome to Vietnam, Corporal Jason Roberts," came from the last degrading voice I ever wanted to hear.

"Oh, shit!" blasted out of my mouth. Thoughts of being shot and left to suffer and eventually die in a pool of my blood filled my mind. Then the thought of turning and running. I couldn't run. In a strange country hundreds of miles from home. I had to stand there and somehow survive.

"Do you recognize me, Corporal?"

"Yes, sir I do."

My left hand clinched my camera case. I pulled it against my side. My right hand pressed hard against my forehead. My heels gave a quick snap together.

The last person I wanted to see in Vietnam stood not ten feet in front of me. I impressed the general whom I wanted to impress with one photograph in the wrong way. The last person I unintentionally wronged stood ready to take revenge on me. It was none other than General William Moorehead III.

For what seemed like an eternity, the General stood there glaring at me. His jaw muscles twitched. I could only imagine the General wanted to see me thrown into hell and burn for eternity.

I had accepted being sent to Vietnam as punishment for sending the General's wife the photograph. I did not expect General Moorehead to be here as well. Now my short life expectancy just got shorter. That day I seriously pondered the thought of committing suicide.

As my right hand lowered, I felt like I should say something. "Corporal Jason Roberts, combat photographer reporting as ordered, sir."

The General wasn't impressed. He circled me with both his hands clutched behind his back. I waited, expecting to feel the General's hand or a hard object land against the back of my head. Nothing happened.

The General came around to my front. "So, fate has brought us together again. You brought an end to my marriage when you sent that photo to my wife. In addition, the Joint Chiefs took away one of my hard-earned stars, resulting in setting my career back ten years. Now, it is my mission to make your life a living hell, or worse."

I opened my mouth to explain, but I closed it. I remained silent. It had been several months. I couldn't think of saying anything that would appease his anger. So, I didn't try.

THE ORDERS

"Let me tell you something, Corporal Roberts. Central Command will not put you directly under my direct command. However, if I see your camera pointing in a direction other than at the enemy, I will grab the nearest M16 and unload a full clip into your sorry ass. Do I make myself clear?"

"Yes, sir, yes, sir, May I say something, sir?" Stupid me. I wanted to justify my actions before the General.

Turning his back to me, he took a couple of steps. "Go ahead, you can't get yourself into any deeper shit with me. "

"With all due respect, sir, I thought the woman you were kissing was your wife. I thought it would be a delightful Christmas gift for you and your wife to have a framed picture…"

"Stop right there!" General Moorehead's face turned red. I expected him to have a heart attack. "That is no excuse, soldier. You should not be taking a picture of a superior officer without that officer's express permission."

The General took a few deep breaths. I could tell he was getting ready to tell me about his little plan for me. "I have arranged for you to spend the rest of your time in the Army where I could see you suffer. Special arrangements have been made. You are assigned to the craziest Long-Range Recon squad in this lousy country. You will serve alongside some of the most seasoned suicidal misfits this United States Military has ever had. Your new squad leader has been given orders to place you as his second. I have been told members of this squad will shoot anyone in their squad who screws up."

The General stopped, turned, and placed his index finger one inch from my nose. "As much as I want to see your sorry ass lying dead in the middle of that airfield, out there bleeding to death." His index finger pointed out the door. "And see you getting run over by a C-130. In all fairness, I am giving you one out. I have been told you have about a year on your enlistment before you can go stateside on reserve duty. If you survive one full year in his country. I will see you get a discharge of less than honorable."

"What is the catch?" I asked.

"I see your primary MOS is a photographer. Your secondary is infantry. You will need to shoot something other than with your camera to stay alive. I still want you to send me three wonderful photos back to Central Command each week. Those photos will be part of your squad's operational performance reports.

In the meantime, I confined you to this shack until your new sergeant arrives. He will take you to your new unit. As a warning, he does not keep a regular schedule. He may show up later today or tomorrow or in a couple of days. In the meantime, I confine you to this Quonset hut.

"If you leave this hut without an escort, you will be considered a deserter." The General concluded with a devilish grin. "There is a standing order to shoot you on sight."

He then walked past me with his shoulder bumping hard against mine. On the way out, he slammed the screen door so hard. It bounced open and closed twice. I thought the door was going to fall off its hinges.

I heard the jeep drive off. I picture my duffel bag still in the back. Lost gear meant more trouble. When I peeked out the door, my heart jumped, there on the ground ten feet from me, my duffel bag. I looked around, but no one was in sight. I took the risk, ran out, grabbed my duffel bag, and ran back inside.

While I looked around, I pictured spending the next several days in that galvanized oven. My uniform became soaked with sweat. Wooden crates were stacked along one wall with a layer of cardboard boxes on top. Against the opposing wall stretched a thin mattress and two wool blankets folded neatly.

I began my incarceration by reading the labels on the crates and boxes. The labels ranged from meal rations, medical supplies, and a couple of boxes labeled body bags. I was thankful for the meal rations. At least, it meant I would not starve while waiting to get escorted out of there.

MEET PSYCHO

I slid one crate next to that thin mattress and used it as a nightstand. I spent the time checking out how my cameras weathered during my trip halfway around the world. Then, without warning, the Quonset hut door flew open. A loud bellowing voice said, "I am looking for a Corporal Jason Roberts."

I jumped to attention and turned toward the doorway. A five-foot ten-inch man in his late twenties dressed in a flowery shirt and shorts stood in the doorway.

I gave him a quick salute. "Yes, sir, that's me. Corporal Jason Roberts Combat Photographer."

"They call me Sergeant Psycho. I'm your psychopathic combat sergeant and squad leader."

Not knowing how to respond, I just stood there. Hearing Psycho's introduction, my hope of surviving the year evaporated.

Psycho didn't dress like what I would have expected. His slicked-back hair, wearing a flowery Hawaiian short-sleeved shirt hanging over his waist. His pants legs cut off above his knees and leather sandals gave me the impression we were going to go to a party.

Psycho took his time examining me. I could feel his eyes slowly go from my head to my feet and then back up again. The whole time, he didn't smile. Then, out of the blue, he asked, "Do you have anything else to wear besides your Army duds?"

"I just have an extra set of my issue in my bag."

"I mean civvies. Like jeans and a casual shirt. You can keep those boots on. Where we will be going, you will need some other clothes. It looks like we are going to need to make a stop at this place I know before we go for a beer or two."

That was the last thing I expected to hear from my new sergeant. "Sir, I didn't expect I would need any other type of clothes."

"Before I can take you into the jungle or introduce you to the squad, I have to teach you a few things."

"I finished my Advance Combat Training."

"If you follow that training, you will be dead in a month. It looks like I am going to have to teach you how to stay alive."

Psycho paused. "Since I have a couple of chores to perform before introducing you to the squad. I will have to take you with me. We're going to Saigon. While there, I will school you on the important stuff."

"With all respect, sir, General Moorehead ordered me to stay here until you took me to meet the squad."

Psycho smiled, "What the General doesn't know won't hurt him or you. Our first stop in Saigon will be this little shop I know. I can't have you looking like a cherry soldier. If you look like a tourist, you will be less likely to get shot."

Psycho headed for the door. I reached for my bag. Psycho turned and said, "Leave it. You'll be spending the night here."

As we got in his Jeep; I tried to remind Psycho about the orders the General gave me. I have caused enough trouble. The last thing I wanted was to get my new sergeant in trouble. Psycho ignored me while driving around the base and pointing out specific buildings and their importance.

By the time we were heading out the main gate, I gave up trying to remind Psycho about the weight of the General's orders. I could tell Psycho's only goal was to get me ready before meeting the squad. As we left Tan Son Nhut, I wondered what Psycho's plans were for getting me ready.

THE MAN THE MYTH

I don't think I ever heard of Psycho's real name. All I know is he went by one of three names: Sarge, Psycho, or Sergeant Psycho.

After I finally met Psycho's squad, I heard a lot of stories about Psycho. The rumors started back in the States. Psycho heard they were sending troops to Vietnam. He wanted to go so badly that he escaped from the mental hospital and tried to join the Marine Corps, but they rejected him. They said he was too crazy for them. So, he went over to see the Army recruiter. They signed him up on the spot. The next day, the Army shipped him off to Fort Ord for boot camp. After boot camp, he volunteered for Vietnam.

Psycho went from a private to sergeant in less than a year. I heard from a couple of guys in another squad that Psycho stole the sergeant stripes off a dead soldier. He put them on and refused to take them off. He did such a good job killing the Viet Cong and keeping American soldiers alive; they let him keep the stripes. Eventually, everyone accepted Psycho as a sergeant.

Regardless of Psycho's craziness, he lost no one in his squad, except those who didn't follow his orders. I even heard those who didn't follow Psycho's orders would get shot by him.

As time went on, I found out no officer or enlisted man wanted to go on a mission with him. Psycho was vehemently opposed to retreating. He believed if you attacked hard and fast enough, the enemy would go running or surrender.

It didn't matter how deep in the jungle or if he had air or artillery support or not. He had a mission, and he was going to complete it. The North Vietnamese called his squad The Devils. Among American and South Vietnamese soldiers, it was known as C4. After the plastic explosive personality of its members. Both the Viet Cong and the North Vietnamese Army had a bounty on his head and a lesser bounty on each of his squads. That only boosted Psycho's ego. I believe it only made Psycho fight harder.

SURVIVAL 101

P sycho drove past the main gate at Tan Son Nhut for about a mile before he pulled onto the side of the road. He reached under his seat, pulled out a semi-automatic handgun in a shoulder holster, and handed it to me.

For a moment, I stared at it. I didn't expect to be issued a sidearm so soon. Psycho had handed me a non-regulation Army sidearm. He handed me a Browning Hi-Powered 35 millimeter otherwise known as the BHP-35. I didn't know at the time that handgun had the reputation for being one of the most reliable nine-millimeter semi-automatics of its day. It held a 13-round magazine and accurately hit a target over fifty yards away. After learning its potential, I understood why Psycho handed it to me and everyone in the squad carried one.

"Put it on. You may need it," Psycho ordered.

I took the holster and gun. I leaned forward in my seat and fitted the holster belt around my waist and put the shoulder strap over my shoulder. Then I checked the BHP-35. Psycho instructed me to put a round in the chamber and make sure the safety was on. Then I put it in the holster and snapped the cover flap down.

"Why did you want me to make sure there is a round in the chamber?" I asked.

"You never know when you need to defend yourself. This entire country is one big war zone." Psycho looked down at my holster. "Did you double-check the safety?"

I nodded. "Yes, with the safety on and the flap is secure."

Psycho grinned. He put the Jeep in gear, and we were off to Saigon.

"Sir, are you expecting trouble while we are in Saigon?"

"Since Tet, this entire country is one big combat zone. You may be classified as a photographer, but if you want to get out of here alive, you will need to kill or be killed. No matter who is pointing a gun at you. It doesn't matter if you are in the jungle on a mission or taking a shower in the barracks. Have that sidearm with you. You will never know when you will need it."

While Psycho drove the jeep, I kept my eyes straightforward and nodded at the end of every other sentence. Every muscle in my body could not get any tighter from the fear I felt.

After entering the city limits of Saigon, Psycho continued with his lessons. They took on a tone that included a doubt about me measuring up. "Let me tell you here and now. I don't like the idea of escorting around some green cherry soldier. You don't have any actual combat experience. You have the label of a combat photographer. In my book, you are a liability to me and my squad.

I know in Germany; you pissed off General Moorehead in a way that sent waves clear to the Pentagon. Your picture-taking forced the Joint Chiefs to take away one of General Moorehead's stars and send him to this godforsaken place. I still have trouble understanding how he could cut orders for you to be my second. The only thing I can think of is that he must think I will get so frustrated with you that I will shoot you myself."

WHO SHOOTS FIRST

Psycho parked the jeep in front of a little clothing shop on the edge of the business district of Saigon. The shop specialized in providing clothes for off-duty soldiers. The shop stocked cheap clothes of decent quality.

Before I could get out of the Jeep, Psycho looked me in the eye and said, "Before we go inside, there are a few basic rules you must never break." I couldn't imagine what else he wanted me to know.

"If you violate any of my basic rules, I will shoot you myself. It won't be a flesh wound. I will aim directly right between your pretty brown eyes. Do you understand?"

I nodded, shaking in fear. "Yes, sir."

"You will carry that sidearm at all times. You are going to point it in the direction I tell you. You will shoot the VC (Viet Cong), or the NVA (North Vietnamese Army), or any communist sympathizer I tell you to shoot."

Pointing to my holster continued his list of rules. "That nine-millimeter Browning that is under your arm will be your principal weapon when on or off patrol. Before leaving on patrol, we will issue you a special assault rifle. It will be your responsibility to keep it in excellent working order.

Have you had any training on an AK-47?"

"No, sir."

After meeting the squad, I will ensure you are fully checked out on their use. I want you to be able to use one when required. There will be times when we will be in the field and are running low on ammo. We will take an AK from a dead North Vietnamese along with some of their ammo and use it against them.

How good of a shot are you?"

"I made Marksman, sir."

"Good, the way we operate here is, if you shoot and kill the enemy, that is okay. If you shoot and wound him in a way that makes him scream in pain, that's even better. The enemy screaming in pain will put fear in the minds of his comrades. If you wound him, his comrades have to run to him and pull him out of a firefight. Great.

We want the VC to waste time and manpower on their wounded. That makes them easier targets. Do you understand these rules?"

"Yes, sir. I do," I said, pushing the words out of my throat past my lips.

"Everyone in the squad, except you, has had at least one tour of duty under their belt. We will leave you behind before taking time to babysit you. If we have to, we will let the VC babysit you or kill you for us."

"What about my assignment to take pictures?" I asked nervously.

"Only after the bullets have stopped flying, and the area is secure, I will let you take pictures. I will not have any member of my squad risk their life, so you can get some award-winning photographs.

Hell, I'll even let you take my picture. Just make sure you get my good side." Psycho smiled while tapping his index finger on his right cheek.

Now let's go inside and get you some proper civics."

Psycho picked out a Hawaiian-style shirt, khaki shorts, and a white cowboy hat. The shirt had a pattern of red cherries. I felt like that outfit made me stand out more than blend into the surroundings. I couldn't complain too much because he paid for the lot.

When we got back in the jeep, Psycho proceeded to give me a tour of Saigon. I sat overwhelmed in the passenger seat, while he pointed out places. I felt he expected me to remember each one. They included the American Embassy, Independence Plaza, and the Cholon district. Psycho scared me the way he took that jeep in and out of bicycles and people walking. A handful of cars and military vehicles seem to give way to our jeep. The whole time, Psycho emphasized how unsafe for any soldier to be in Saigon alone.

When our jeep turned onto another street, I had to push back the fear of being shot at by the Viet Cong or Sergeant Psycho. I had heard that getting shot would be quite painful. I didn't want to have that experience.

At that point in my life, I had never shot another individual. The idea of inflicting pain and suffering on another human being made me sick. If I didn't follow Psycho's orders, he would shoot or kill me. When I joined the Army, I didn't expect to be put into that kind of situation.

DRINKING WITH PSYCHO

As the day's shadows from the buildings reached across the street. Psycho parked the Jeep. We walked a half block to this little sidewalk cafe that doubled as a bar. Regardless of how relaxed everything looked, I felt the tension in the air. Off in the distance, I could hear gunfire. The gunfire didn't seem to bother Psycho. He had us sit at a table next to the sidewalk. Two other tables extended out onto the sidewalk.

A waiter came out to take our orders. Psycho ordered us beers without asking for my approval. His only comment to me was, "The beer is the best beer made and sold in all of Vietnam."

Psycho's eyes kept going toward this Vietnamese man sitting at the far table. Dressed in a faded tan shirt and black pants, he seemed like a local relaxing while drinking a late afternoon beer.

The waiter brought our first round. Psycho spoke to the waiter in Vietnamese. A few minutes later, the waiter brought two small shot glasses filled with clear liquid. He set one shot glass in front of me and the second one in front of Psycho.

I looked down at my shot glass, then up at Psycho. In my short drinking career, the only hard liquor I ever drank was tequila. What set in that shot glass looked and smelled more dangerous?

"Drink up, young man," Psycho said, nudging the shot glass closer toward me. "It is the best local moonshine in the country. If you down the shot glass fast and follow it with the beer, you will live."

I grabbed my shot glass in one hand and my beer in the other. As fast as I could, I poured the shot glass contents down my throat. Before my tongue could register the taste, I flooded my mouth with the beer. In less than a minute, a warm feeling rushed through my body. The tension I once felt evaporated, followed by increasing blurred vision and dying brain cells. Many of my fears floated off into the nether land. I felt a flood of euphoric confidence.

Now feeling brave enough, I asked Psycho, "How did you get the name of Psycho?"

Psycho just grinned at me. He took another sip from his beer glass. He looked down at the table, then looked up at me. "I'll tell you a story that is told about me. It was one of many that keep my reputation alive."

"There is more than one incident that got you your name?" I asked.

"Yes, the one I liked was escaping from the mental hospital."

"What about when you got to Vietnam?"

"It was during my first tour of duty. I was in the country for maybe six months. The unit I was attached to had the job of securing an LZ (Landing Zone) for a portion of the 9th Marine Expeditionary Brigade. A group of Huey's were to unload the Marines. The Marines were to start a surprise offensive about ten clicks east of the Cambodian border. Just minutes before their Hueys were to come over the treetops, this water buffalo wandered into the middle of the LZ. He started munching on the green grass like he owned the clearing.

I heard the first Hueys coming over the treetop. I grabbed the sniper's rifle and shot the water buffalo dead."

"Why would they name you Psycho over that?"

Psycho's grin got bigger. "The next day, I was called into this colonel's office. He read me the riot act for shooting the property of a South Vietnamese citizen. Now the United States had to pay the owner of the water buffalo for me killing it. The Colonel asked me why in the hell I shot the water buffalo.

I politely conveyed to the Colonel we had reliable intelligence the water buffalo was a Viet Cong sympathizer. The water buffalo had the assignment to stop the Marines from landing in that clearing. The buffalo's action confirmed this when he wandered into the middle of the LZ. The Colonel looked at me, shook his head, and said, I had to be Psycho to think he was going to believe me."

I picked up my beer glass and pretended to take a long drink, suppressing my laughter.

That evening, sitting in the middle of Saigon, at a street cafe/bar. Across the table from me was a crazy Sargent who bore the nickname Psycho. In the background, I heard the Beatles' song, "Penny Lane." I felt like I had landed in a nightmarish version of *Alice in Wonderland*.

PSYCHO AT WORK

Psycho kept taking glances over my right shoulder. My curiosity heightened each time I noticed Psycho's eyes shooting off in that direction. I started to turn and look at what caught his attention. I felt a hard tap on the table. Psycho frowned and said, "No!" He motioned for me to lean forward.

I leaned forward and asked. "What is so important about that guy sitting behind me?"

Psycho leaned toward me. "He is a cook at the American Embassy. He has been passing information to North Vietnamese spies. This place is known for being a place where spies hang out."

Psycho reached out his hand toward me. "Let me see your sidearm."

I gave Psycho a questioning look. "Now?"

"Now!" He ordered. His index finger tapped on the table.

I reached into my holster and pulled out my weapon. I could not imagine why Psycho would want to see my weapon when he had given it to me hours before. My mind flashed back to barroom shootouts from the John Wayne movies. I dismissed that from happening here.

I went to set my weapon on the table with the barrel pointing between Psycho and me. Psycho grabbed my hand. His thumb flicked the safety off. He turned the barrel toward me. I moved my body to the left so the barrel would not be pointing at me.

The next thing I heard was a pop, and my wrist yanked from the recoil. A painful scream came from behind me. I immediately knew where the bullet had landed.

Psycho leaped up from his chair. "What the hell! Didn't I tell you about keeping the safety on?"

I sat there, stunned. I was getting blamed for what Psycho had just done.

The cries of pain and the choice of Vietnamese words filled that bar. I turned to see that supposed Vietnamese spy gripping his arm. Fiery red daggers shot from burning red anger in his eyes.

I jumped up. My sidearm clutched in my hand. Smoke coming out of the barrel. I flicked the safety back on, stuffed it in my holster, and latched the flap.

Psycho ran to the spy's aid. Turning back toward me, Psycho yelled at me so loudly that the gathering onlookers could hear without a doubt. "I told you to be careful. I can't believe you are so clumsy. You have gone and shot this guy. All because you were lazy enough to not put the safety on. Lucky for you, you have only wounded him. Still, I have to attend to his wound."

"Sir, Psycho, I didn't mean to, but when you grab…" Before I could get any more words out of my mouth, Psycho was kneeling next to the guy, putting a bar towel around his wound.

Psycho turned back to me and winked. He mouthed the words, "Just follow my lead."

The poor guy would not stop screaming at us in a mixture of English and Vietnamese. One thing I knew for sure was he did not want to order us a round of beer.

Psycho ripped the guy's shirt sleeve above where the bullet

hit his arm. The waiter ran over with a couple more bar towels to reduce the bleeding and wrap the wound.

The local police pushed through the gathering crowd. They questioned me. Psycho stepped between us. "Give the kid a break. It's his first day in the country. He wanted to show me his weapon, and it went off."

The policeman took down our name. A short time later, an ambulance showed up. The policemen had to clear the onlookers so the ambulance attendants could get to their patients. By that time, he appeared more accepting of his injury. The ambulance crew loaded the poor guy into the ambulance and headed for a nearby hospital.

As the ambulance disappeared from view, Psycho put his hand on my shoulder. "It is time for us to go. It's going to be dark soon, and I got to get you back to the airfield. I think we have done enough damage here today."

"Shouldn't we go to the hospital and see how that guy is doing?" I asked.

"No, we have to get ready for tomorrow. We have to take some supplies up north, and I have to introduce you to the rest of the squad. Besides, he's dead by now."

FIRST NIGHT

I didn't say another word until we left the city limits of Saigon. Still, one question kept eating at me. I had to ask. "The bullet went into his arm, and it didn't hit an artery? Shouldn't he still be alive?"

Psycho kept driving with his eyes on the road. "There are two things you should know. One, he was a spy for the North Vietnamese. Two, I had you shoot him so I could get close enough to kill him."

"You didn't kill him. He let out a string of curse words when they loaded him into the ambulance. The bullet only caused a flesh wound in his arm. You even wrapped it to stop the bleeding."

"Trust me, he'll be dead before he gets to the hospital. Bandaging his wound kept his focus on his arm while I used a syringe to inject air into his femoral artery. When the air bubbles reach his heart and brain, he's dead."

All the way back, I could see the smile on Psycho's face. It reminded me of a cat that had eaten the canary. This was another one of those times where I wished I had not taken that picture of General Moorehead and his mistress. I should have listened to the sergeant who warned me. The thought of ever having any Good Vibrations like what the Beach Boys sang seemed so far away.

A hundred yards before the main gate at Tan Son Nhut was this bar. Psycho stopped in front of it. While there, he had me down a couple of shots of Jack Daniels with my beer. He said it would help me sleep. I am sure he saw how my first day in Vietnam left me so overwhelmed and uptight.

We got back to my Quonset prison well past midnight. I remember falling out of the jeep and my lips kissing the ground. I don't remember getting inside.

In the early dawn hours, I pictured being back home. My buddies and me sitting on the tailgate of my truck drinking beers and watching the Fourth of July fireworks. Between explosions, we talked about girls and what we wanted to do with the rest of our lives. I loved how the night sky would light up and balls of light would fall to the ground.

The sound of fireworks exploding in the air and the smell of burned gunpowder filled my nostrils. Wait, a minute! It hit me. I set up and looked around. This was not Idaho. Cardboard and wooden crates surrounded me, and a tin roof peppered with holes overhead. Flashes of light shot through the holes.

Those were not fireworks I was hearing. There were sounds of incoming mortar rounds and machine-gun fire. What I was smelling was exploding mortars and gun smoke. The base was under attack. I felt a couple of rounds zing through that Quonset hut.

The Army had not issued me a rifle yet. I reached for my sidearm. My holster was empty. A thin woolen Army blanket lay beside me. Petrified with fear, I reached over and pulled it over my head, and tried not to move a muscle. I stayed face down. While praying to Almighty God to just let me live through the night.

Like a light switch being turned off. The night abruptly fell into an eerie silence. Faint beams of light flickered through the screen door and holes in the wall. The only sound I could hear was my heart beating. Adrenaline mixed with the blood rushing through my veins. I took labored, slow breaths.

For the rest of the night, I lay awake thinking about my life decisions. My good intentions went so wrong. I wished for a way to make my choices over again.

The more I tried to doze off, the slightest noise caused me to shake in fear for my life. I kept waiting for another round of mortars and gunfire. It didn't.

Time dragged on. I just wanted to make it through the night alive and not wounded. Sometime before dawn, I fell asleep.

DAY TWO

The attempt at opening my eyes only resulted in throbbing pain behind them. The movement of my head reminded me of all the booze I consumed the day before. No matter how I wished for my hangover to go away, it didn't. It took a while before I could keep open my eyes for more than a few seconds.

"I'm so screwed!" came the words out of my mouth as I thought of my first day in South Vietnam. I wished the past few months were a dream. My new sergeant had a handle that matched his craziness. He enjoyed killing someone in the late afternoon at a sidewalk bar.

I attempted to stand up. My legs buckled, and I fell back on the thin mattress. My head spun through the fog. I swore I would never drink that much hard liquor again. That resolution didn't help my current condition.

The thoughts of suicide rose through the pain in my head. Two things kept me from following through. First, my side arm was missing. I hoped I didn't leave it somewhere I shouldn't have. Two, my Sunday School teachers talked about people who commit suicide as going to hell. If hell was worse than what I was experiencing, I didn't want to go there.

I tried to shake off the fog for fear of Sergeant Psycho wanting me to do morning PTs. I feared what he might have in store for me before meeting the squad members. Either way, I didn't want to be hungover when he showed up.

I started reading the labels on the boxes that spent the night with me. One label read MCI. It stood for Military Combat Individual or meals in cans. I opened one to find some canned peaches. I opened one and sat on the mattress, eating them.

As soon as I got the first peach slice in my mouth, the door flew open. Sergeant Psycho made his entrance wearing regular Army greens. He looked down at me. I looked up at him and smiled. I felt like when my mother caught me eating my birthday cake a day early.

"Get up, kid," Psycho ordered. "You deserve to eat better food than that shit. We have a busy day ahead of us. First stop, mess hall. We are going to get some hot food in our guts."

I set the unused can of peaches on a nearby crate and pushed myself off the floor. Then I headed for the door when Psycho stopped me. He put his index finger on my chest. He looked at me from head to toe and back up into my eyes.

"What are you wearing?" He asked.

I looked down at my clothes. I still had on the clothes from the day before.

"You better change into some regular Army fatigues. If you walk into the mess hall looking like that, they will kick you out. You look more like some hungover tourist."

I pulled some clean fatigues out of my duffel bag and changed. I barely got my boots on before Psycho motioned for me to follow him as he headed out the door.

On the way back from the mess hall, we stopped by the motor pool to check out a Deuce in Half. Psycho informed me we would be taking some crates and boxes north with us to Da

Nang. They were the same crates and boxes that kept me company through the night.

I tossed the boxes up to Psycho in the back of the truck. I noticed that three of the boxes had unusual-looking tape sealing them. Three of the boxes had written on them:

LT A. Doyle. OPEN AT YOUR OWN RISK.

"Who is Lieutenant A. Doyle?" I asked.

Psycho stood up straight and said, "Don't ask questions. We will stop by the base hospital. You can meet Lieutenant A. Doyle there. She will be traveling with us to Da Nang. You better get a move on. We need to be in Da Nang before dark."

Those boxes were my first introduction to Lieutenant Doyle. Little did I know that women would be a major factor in staying alive while in Vietnam. She would become someone who I would even depend upon later.

Once we had the deuce and half-loaded, Psycho drove over to the base hospital. He drove around to the back of the loading dock. A sign that read "Morgue" marked a door to the right. Psycho knocked twice, and then it opened. A woman wearing green Army fatigues under a white lab coat invited us inside.

LT DOYLE

To my surprise, Lieutenant A. Doyle was, in fact, Lieutenant Alice Carson Doyle. The only reason I could find was to make my time in Vietnam pleasurable. I didn't care about her being a lieutenant and me being a lonely corporal. Just being around her and seeing her smile made everything else better.

A little over five feet two inches tall. Lieutenant Doyle's shoulder-length black hair and facial features got my heart beating fast every time I came close to her. Being half Japanese and half American gave her a unique perspective on situations.

Her father was an American intelligence officer sent to Japan at the end of WWII. He developed a relationship with her mother, whom he later married. Her mother was from some kind of ancient warrior/assassin clan in Japan known as the Iga. They married and moved to San Francisco wanting a peaceful life and to raise a family. I learned later from the guys in the squad that Lieutenant Doyle came to Vietnam as an intelligence officer posing as a nurse.

On my second day in South Vietnam, Psycho and I followed Lieutenant Doyle down a hallway into a side room. Walls were painted an off-white, and no pictures or posters hung on them. At the far end of the room was a gray metal desk with a swivel chair behind it. In front were two gray metal chairs and a coat rack were the only furniture in the room. I noticed on the floor next to the left wall set two cardboard boxes.

Lieutenant Doyle took off her white lab coat and hung it on the coat rack. She sat behind the desk and took a pencil. Psycho motioned for me to sit in one chair while he set in the other. Lieutenant Doyle spent the next minute or two shuffling papers and writing on some.

I closely watched every move she made. Regardless of her uniform and rank, I found her so captivating by how her jet-black hair hung just above her shoulders. She didn't need any lipstick or makeup. She held the pencil and shuffled the papers like some choreographed production. In my mind, she couldn't be any more beautiful.

"Who is your friend?" Lieutenant Doyle asked, looking up at Psycho while pointing her pencil at me. Her question startled me. I turned red.

"This is the newest member of C4," answered Psycho.

"Is this the photographer I heard about?"

Psycho nodded. "Yes, he's the soldier who caused General Moorehead to lose one of his stars by taking his picture."

"How did you get so lucky to end up with him?"

"The brass must have figured he would be a fitting punishment for both of us. To make things even more difficult for both of us, I have orders to make him my second."

I tried to defend myself by speaking up. "I didn't …"

Lieutenant Doyle put up her hand to stop me. "I don't need to hear your side of the story. You are here. Let us just go on from there."

I could see her eyes inspecting me. "What is your name, soldier?"

"Corporal Jason Roberts, ma'am."

"I see you didn't lose a stripe after you sent the picture to the General's wife."

"No ma'am, they just sent me here. They must have figured that being sent to Vietnam would be enough punishment."

"You listen to Psycho. If anyone can keep you alive, he can. I don't want to see you in my morgue." She said, with no sign of emotion on her face.

"Are those the boxes we are taking with us to Da Nang?" Psycho asked, pointing to the two cardboard boxes sitting on the floor.

"You can take them out to the truck. Make sure they get fastened down. A ride in those C130's can be rough." Doyle looked down at the paperwork in front of her. "I have to make sure all the paperwork is right before we leave. I'll meet the two of you outside."

Lieutenant Doyle soon joined us at the truck. She took the center position between Psycho and me.

The loadmaster drove the truck onto the C130. Psycho and Lieutenant Doyle double-checked the tie-downs the loadmaster made. We took the seats made for ride-a-longs.

The flight from Tan Son Nhut to Da Nang didn't take as long as I wish it had. Lieutenant Doyle spent most of the time schooling me. "We are here to aid the South Vietnam government in an official capacity. Unofficially, we are tasked with stabilizing the region from communist aggression. You will find us doing things that don't make sense. The best thing you can do is just follow orders."

The words Lieutenant Doyle spoke made little sense to me. During the entire flight, I felt nervous sitting next to her. However, the sound of her voice fascinated me. At that time, I didn't understand why one woman had such an effect on me.

Right before landing, she said, "When you meet C4, you will

notice that C4 comprises soldiers from both the Army and Marine Corps."

"I thought Army and Marine units and squads didn't mix?" I blurted out.

"You will find here it doesn't matter what branch of the military you are in. All the branches fight the same enemy. Soldiers who follow regulations don't get assigned to C4. Psycho will follow regulations most of the time. Under his leadership, he causes C4 to accomplish more than those who follow regulations."

Our C130 touched down and taxied to our off-loading area at the airfield. The back ramp lowered. I walked out and stood at the end of the ramp and watched in amazement as soldiers and airmen rushed in different directions. They all seemed like they were going in a specific direction for a specific reason. I had been told that a large number of military operations were launched from Da Nang. The Da Nang Air Base had to be ten times bigger than what I had imagined.

"Hey kid, get the hell out of the way." I heard Psycho yell. I turned to see Psycho driving that truck down the ramp, barely giving me enough time to jump out of the way.

Our first stop was to drop Lieutenant Doyle off at the base morgue. Then we went over to the Hooch assigned to C4. Psycho parked out front and honked with three longs.

MEET THE SQUAD

A row of buildings made of wood with corrugated roofs and surrounded by sandbags stood along the northwestern border of the base. The slang term for those buildings was hooch. Given to other than regulation barracks. That group of hooch housed various soldiers from various units. Charlie Company's fourth squad (aka C4) had the end hooch next to the parameter fence. The other hooches housed other squads that went out on Long-Range Recons, more commonly referred to as LRRPs.

Psycho had his own unique way of introducing me to C4. Psycho jumped into the back of the deuce and handed me the crates we were to unload. I would hand off that crate to one of the squad members. That squad member would introduce themselves.

The first squad member in line stood six foot three inches tall and maybe a hundred and seventy pounds. As I handed him the first wooden crate, he said, "They call me Shadow. If I turn sideways, you are only going to see my shadow. I'm from Indianapolis, Indiana. If you want to talk about cars and racing, I am your man."

Next in line was a much shorter Hispanic soldier. I wondered how he got into the Army for being so short. "My name is Ruben. I was born in LA. I'm known as the squad's Tunnel Rat. If there is a tunnel that needs to be flushed out. I'm the one they send inside."

The third one stepped up and took a cardboard box. He had black hair and bulging muscles. "My name is Mick. I grew up on the streets of New York City. Hell's Kitchen, to be exact. I joined the Marine Corps, but when I got to Nam, I got in a couple of bar fights, then they stuck me with this squad. My job is to show everyone in this squad what a real soldier is like. Hu Rah!"

Next to step up was an average-looking GI with his hair a little long. "I'm Dave the squad's Medic. They busted me with a pound of Mary Jane. The judge gave me the option to either go to jail or join the Army. So, I joined the Army. This squad lets me smoke all I want, as long as I share."

Then there was this soldier with wild eyes and curly red hair. "My name is James. Everyone here calls me Sparky. My lot in life is to blow things up. I don't just blow things up. I make each explosion a piece of creative artistry."

After Sparky carried his box into the Hooch, a fit black man took a box from my hands. "My name is Leroy. I'm from Georgia. After my first enlistment, the people of Georgia didn't give me no respect. So, I re-enlisted. I'm the squad's sniper. A damm good one at that."

Last but not least, a middle-aged Vietnamese man stepped up for his box. "My name is Pham. Everyone around here calls me Fame. I'm the squad's translator and guide. During downtime, I sing Elvis Presley and Johnny Cash songs to whoever will listen.

A North Vietnamese Army came to my village, killed my family, and left me for dead. These men saved my life. They even helped me kill those who killed my family. Now C4 is my family."

I took the last box and followed C4 inside. I found them standing around, waiting for me to introduce myself. "My name is Corporal Jason Roberts. My main MOS is Combat Photographer. I took a picture of General Moorehead with a lady and sent it to his wife. Instead of putting me before a firing squad, they sent me here. This is my first time in a combat zone."

Mick pointed to an empty bunk. "That's yours."

"What about the gear sitting on it?" I asked.

"Take it back to the storeroom. We'll take it to get shipped back to the States and the soldier's family, tomorrow."

"What happened to him?"

"A young Marine got assigned to us. He lasted two missions before he caught a bullet." Ruben said.

"Hopefully you will last longer than Louis," Mick added.

TRAINING DAYS

Eight cubbies occupied the back third of the Hooch. Next to the back door is a large, locked closet. Each man had an assigned cubby for his gear. The closet stored the ammo and explosives to be taken on missions.

After mess the next morning, each man brought me something I would need for when we went on missions. I placed them in my cubby.

Dave brought me a first-aid pouch. "If you ever get wounded, I won't have to go looking for medical supplies to help you. You will have them on you."

Ruben brought me a backpack. "You will carry all your supplies in here. It will be full before we leave on a mission."

Mick brought me a flak vest. "This will give you some protection from flying bullets. If you get hit, it will sting, but you will be alive. You will get issued another one when we get back to base."

Leroy handed me five pairs of new socks and a roll of toilet paper. "These are the essentials for every mission."

Shadow gave me a K-bar knife. "Be careful with this. I have just finished sharpening it."

Pham gave me four carabiners and a three hundred feet of climbing rope. "You never know when you need to climb up or repel down."

Psycho introduced me to the weapons closet. He pointed at one section. "This is your section. In here, you will keep your rifle, ammo clips, and any other explosives you will be carrying."

Over the next couple of days, I spent a lot of time getting to know how C4 operated. Most of the time were at different firing ranges. Psycho had us shoot ten rounds sitting and standing along with another five with our sidearms. What C4 taught me never got mentioned in basic or when I took Advance Combat Training. What they did and how they did things were different. All I knew was it kept them alive. They executed every little detail flawlessly.

With packs filled with rocks, we would march single file to the first firing range. Psycho insisted that I shoot at specific places on the target. No more firing at center mass or spraying a group of bullets in the general direction of the target. Psycho called it a waste of ammunition. When we were in the field on a mission, every bullet had to hit a specific target.

Each member of C4 was already an expert marksman or better. At the firing range, Leroy and Mick would take turns giving me pointers. It didn't take long before my accuracy improved.

After we shot off ten rounds at the first range, Psycho called for a Huey. I started to climb into the back of the Huey. Psycho grabbed me by the collar and pulled me back. We were not to ride in the back. Psycho motioned for the pilot to take off. It hovered approximately thirty feet off the ground, then the Huey's gunner dropped several ropes. As the Huey hovered overhead, we clipped on to them. Then the Huey would lift all of us off the ground and fly us to another location.

We would shoot off another ten rounds. The Huey would show up, drop the ropes, and lift us to another firing range. We repeated this routine three more times. At the last location, we were five miles away from our hooch. Psycho led a force back.

On the second day repeated the same process as we did on the first day. When we got back to the hooch after eating dinner, I asked Shadow, "Why do we train so much?

Shadow grinned and said. "The more time you spend training, the more likely you will not die." Then he walked over to Ruben and tapped him on the head as he walked to the rear of our hooch.

Ruben took a few steps, turned, and yelled, "Beer time! Any of you guys thirsty?" Everyone stopped what they were doing and followed Ruben out through the back door.

I stayed lying on my bunk. After those two days of training, all I wanted to do was sleep. Psycho came over and grabbed one of my legs and pulled me off my bunk. "Beer time! Everyone drinks together. No hanging back and sleeping."

BEER TIME

I walked out the back door of the Hooch. The guys were sitting around a makeshift picnic table. Leroy looked up at me and raised a can of Hamm's beer. "Grab a beer or be square." He then pointed to the coolers at one end of the table.

Everyone gathered around the table. Psycho waited until everyone had got halfway through their beer. He looked over at me and said, "We have this tradition on the night before we go on any mission."

I took a sip from my beer, expecting some kind of hazing tradition.

Dave reached over and offered me a hit off his hand-rolled joint. I put up my hand and shook my head no. "I prefer to get my buzz from beer."

Psycho continued, "I got the unofficial word. We are going to be sent out tomorrow. To keep our tradition, which seems to bring us good luck." Psycho looked over at me. "We gather and discuss what we are going to tell the VC if we ever get captured."

As soon as Psycho said the word, "Captured", my mind flashed to being hung upside down and whipped with a bamboo stick. Just as my fears of impending pain and death subsided, Psycho had to say something to bring it all back.

I did not sign up to get captured and be tortured by the Viet Cong or the North Vietnamese. I wanted to be a professional photographer. The idea of being tortured and spending years in the Hanoi Hilton frightened me.

Psycho looked over at me. "Take a hit off of Dave's joint and release the smoke slowly. It will help calm your nerves."

Psycho and all C4 waited and watched while I took a hit off the joint and slowly released it.

Psycho stared directly at me and continued. "None of us plan on getting captured. This is a precautionary measure that we take. We then have a story to give the Viet Cong. We can give them some misinformation that is believable. If our story is believable enough, we won't get tortured as much. They may let down their guard and we can escape.

Our little tradition seems to have a positive effect. Everyone seems to fight harder when the need arises. This tradition has kept all squad members safe. The only ones we lost were the ones who didn't listen to me."

Looking over at Mick. Psycho asked. "Mick, you were down talking to some of the MAC-V guys. What did they say about our mission?"

Mick took a sip of his beer and cleared his throat. "They told me we will be looking for branches off the Ho Chi Minh Trail. I picked up a rumor. Some Chinese advisors, along with some Chinese troops, have been traveling with the regular North Vietnamese Army. If Chairman Mao has placed troops with the NVA, we are to confirm it."

Psycho nodded with a grin. "In other words, we just might see some action on our terms."

Then Psycho looked over at me. "Jason, since this will be your first real combat mission, I want you to carry the radio and stick close to me." Psycho tapped his right shoulder with his left hand. "This is my right side."

"I thought I was going to be radio man and your number two?" Mick piped up.

"That was the plan, but orders came down from Captain Phillips."

"Since when do we let the brass dictate how we run our squad?"

"They are putting pressure on me to keep the kid in harm's way. I think he has had a string of bad luck. Maybe we can make a real soldier out of him."

"I don't like it. I should be your number two, regardless of what the brass says." Mick said.

Dave injected, "Give the kid a break. The safest place he can be is next to Psycho."

"That is not true. Remember, Psycho has a bounty on his head from the North Vietnamese Army. Being next to Psycho is not really a safe place for him to be," Sparky said.

"Let's not forget that each one of us has a bounty on our heads. The bounty is not as big as Psycho's but a bounty, nevertheless." Ruben injected.

Dave saw I had shown more signs of nervousness. "Now stop scaring the kid. I don't want him fainting the first time we touch down in an LZ."

Laughter and harsh remarks came from everyone in the squad.

Pounding on the table with his empty can of beer, Psycho regained everyone's attention. "Let's get down to business. Anyone got an idea as to what we tell the slant eyes if we get captured?"

Leroy spoke up, "How about the story we had planned last time we went out? The one where we are deserting and looking for asylum in North Vietnam. The only reason we were shooting at them was because they wouldn't listen and started shooting at us first. When they trust us, we can gain some serious intel."

"I like that," said Psycho. "I'll let the Central Command North know it is our way of staying in the fight if any of us gets captured. I haven't received the official time we are to head out. It will most likely be midday or later."

IT IS GETTING REAL

Orders didn't come through until late in the morning. At fifteen hundred hours, two Hueys had their blades turning, waiting to take us to our LZ (Landing Zone). Earlier that day, Psycho sent the squad over to the shooting range for some last-minute practice. He sent me over to the communication center. Since I was to carry the radio, I needed to get the codes and call signs for our mission. Changing codes before each mission prevented the North Vietnamese Army from knowing what we were up to.

I walked in the door to Central Command North. My eyes got fixed on the same captain, wearing a wrinkle-free uniform who met me at Ta Sun Nhut. He stood over a radio operator. He gave me a quick, demeaning glance and continued listening in on a radio conversation.

A Staff Sergeant came up to me and handed me a card with the radio frequencies for C4. In addition, they gave me the call sign of Cameraman.

He reviewed the radio procedures with me. No surprise that C4 got the call sign of Psych Ward. Dust Off meant we needed a medical evacuation of the wounded. Central Command North had the call sign of North Star. They gave me a secret passcode. If there was any suspicion regarding the caller's identity, the passcode would prompt a request for the code.

As I was on my way out the door, the duty sergeant yelled at me. I turned. He pointed to a field radio sitting by his desk. "Hey, Cameraman, don't forget your PRC-77."

"Yes, sir," I said with a salute.

A tube VHF/FM transceiver, the PRC-77, ran off a fifteen-volt battery. I hated that whip antenna. It acted as a flag, signaling my location. Mick showed me how to keep it bent over when not using the radio. If I needed to have the radio on for any length of time, I would tie a branch with leaves to the antenna.

With the radio hanging off my shoulder, I headed out the door when I heard the duty sergeant yell again, "Wait a minute. I have a few more things for you."

The sergeant handed me two bags. One had a couple of extra batteries, and in the other, different colored smoke grenades. I clipped a couple of smoke grenades to the side of the radio for quick access.

Back at the Hooch, I weighed the radio, extra batteries, and smoke grenades. It came to just over twenty pounds. After piling the rest of my gear onto the storage room scale. It tipped to over ninety-five pounds. Then I noticed I forgot to add my camera, camera case, and some film to the pile. That pile included the radio, extra battery, smoke grenades, camera, film, flak vest, sidearm, ammo, canteen, food, first aid kit, and socks. I didn't like the idea of carrying over ninety-five pounds on my back for a week or more.

Sparky walked into the storage room. I looked at him. "Do all of you carry such a heavy pack?"

"Suck it up. You will be all muscle or dead by the end of your first couple of missions."

Sparky must have seen the hopeless look on my face when he

smiled. "Before we leave, we look over what each of us carries. We distribute our loads so each of us carries roughly the same weight. Like Leroy helps me with carrying claymores and ammo. Ruben, Shadow, and Mick carry extra ammo and food."

The butterflies in my stomach subsided a little when we headed for the Hueys and my first mission. We loaded onto our specific Huey in a specific order. Offloading went in reverse order.

In the jungle, C4 walked signal file along a trail. Psycho had me walk third in line behind him. During landings and extractions, I was to be the last on the ground and first in the chopper. C4 practiced communicating with hand signals. Psycho and every man on the squad knew exactly where everyone else would be at any given time.

Since I carried the radio, I could talk on the radio. Then only as close to a whisper, but loud enough for those on the other end of the radio, could hear me. I had a set of earphones that I hung around my neck to hear incoming messages. My communication with the other squad members was to be done with hand signals.

We all got back from the noon mess. Psycho called us all together. "We are going on a little hike for about a week. Pack your gear accordingly." Psycho looked at me and said, "Normally, radio communication with HQ will be only at our LZ and right before our extraction. On this mission, it will be only when I tell you."

MISSION OUTLINE

I blurted out, "What about hot showers and getting mail?" Those words no sooner left my mouth than I realized how dumb they were. I suppose I used it as a means to suppress the fear of getting wounded or killed.

I heard a chuckle from all the guys behind me. Psycho looked at me like he couldn't believe what he heard. "You will have to wait until we get back to take a shower. They will hold your mail until we get back. While we are in the jungle, put up with your own body odor and everyone else's."

I cringed at the thought of suffering through the heat and humidity and not taking a shower. My mother's words of cleanliness, being next to godliness, only emphasized I was in a godless war in a godless country.

Taking a quick breath, Psycho continued. "Now our little hike will be in two parts. The first part of our mission will take place a few clicks after we are dropped off. We are to secure half of the parameter of a clearing. The other half will be done by the third squad. Charlie Company's First and Second squads will be in charge of the clearing itself."

"Is this one of Captain Phillips' little barbecues?" Leroy asked.

"Yes, it is," snapped Psycho. "HQ wants it well protected. Roberts, since you got the radio, you will act as traffic controller under my direction. I will be giving you a signal as to what to say on the radio."

"What is this Captain Phillips barbecue?" I asked.

Mick injected. "Our beloved Captain Phillips goes out of his way to impress visiting congressman and senators by having these barbecues in the jungle. This is his way of demonstrating to visitors what we have done in securing South Vietnam from communist aggression."

Dave had to add more detail. "The Captain uses first and second squads for cooking and entertainment. The third and fourth squads get tasked with security and cleanup. Basically, we sit back in the jungle and watch while they put on this barbecue."

"Isn't what Captain Phillips is doing, against regulations?" I asked.

Leroy added. "Exceptions are always present when it concerns Captain Phillips. It doesn't matter if it is in regulations or not."

Psycho brought the conversation back on track. "The second part of our mission involves a little hike to scout for the North Vietnamese Army coming in from Laos. If we find any sign of supplies or troop movement coming off the Ho Chi Minh Trail, we are going to let Sparky do some of his creative work.

We are going to let Mister Roberts take some pictures so the brass and folks back home can see what kind of work we do. If he can get some pictures of supplies being moved on one of those trails, that would be great.

Get busy getting your shit together. Make sure each one of you brings as much ammo as you can. I don't want us running out of ammo during a firefight. We leave a couple of hours before sunset. A hundred yards from our LZ will be our first sleepover."

After Psycho dismissed the squad, I went to my cubbyhole to grab my gear. I looked all over. I double-checked and triple-checked. Something was missing. I checked it again. Then a light bulb went on in my brain. A vital piece of equipment didn't exist. How could I defend myself without my rifle? What I used in practice was gone. The gun on my hip would not be enough. I could not leave without that one important piece of equipment!

IMPORTANT PIECE MISSING

I tracked down Psycho behind the Hooch. I found him sitting at the table and bent over a map. His eyes moved from one sector to the next. I learned later Psycho would memorize every step of our patrol area before each mission.

"Where is my M16?" I asked. Breaking his concentration.

Psycho's head tilted sideways toward me. "What is your problem?" Then he went back to studying the map.

"The M16 I was using during training is missing. The only weapon I have is the sidearm you gave me back in Saigon."

Looking up at me, he smiled. "I forgot. You need to go to the morgue and see Lieutenant Doyle. She has a present waiting for you."

"Why?" I asked. The thought flashed through my mind. Why would Psycho send me to the morgue to get my own body bag and not a rifle? Did he expect me to get killed on my first mission? My confidence in living through that mission dropped to zero. Getting a M16 at the morgue didn't make any sense to me. I had learned no matter how strange something sounded, if Psycho said, "Do it," I had to do it. He had his reason. Even if it meant several days later before I found out why.

At the door of the morgue, I knocked. From inside, I heard a voice saying, "Enter." I walked inside to see Lieutenant Doyle with another officer sitting on stools next to a workbench, studying some paperwork. The knot in my gut just got bigger. I had hoped to see Lieutenant Doyle alone before I left.

The other officer wore a ball cap with an embroiled silver eagle right above the cap's brim. I had to stop a moment and wonder, "Why would a Bird Colonel be in the morgue talking to Lieutenant Doyle?"

I walked up to them and saluted both of them. Turning toward Lieutenant Doyle, "My sergeant sent me over here to pick up something for our mission." I was afraid if I said the wrong thing, both Lieutenant Doyle and I would be in trouble. I wanted to give Lieutenant Doyle enough information so she would know why I was there, but not get us in trouble.

"Oh, yes," she responded with a smile of acknowledgment. "First, let me introduce you to Colonel Beck. He handles intel gathering through non-traditional sources."

Colonel Beck looked over at me and said, "I understand you have a habit of taking some fascinating photographs. I trust the pictures you take while in Nam will be a benefit to our efforts here."

"That is my intention, sir."

Lieutenant Doyle stood up and walked toward the door of an adjacent room. "Follow me."

She excused herself from the Colonel. I followed her into the storeroom. She pointed at a cardboard box with no markings other than some black faded numbers.

"Take the whole box. In the middle of the body bags, you will find a CAR-15 for you."

Desired by special forces, the CAR-15 was more compact compared to the M16. Having a 10-inch barrel gave it an effective range of 440 yards. Being much quieter and with a lower muzzle flash than the M16 made it the ideal weapon. The standard ammo clip carried 30 rounds.

Lieutenant Doyle placed her hand on top of the box as I held it. "The guys at C4 will fill you in on the details of how to use it. All the guys prefer the CAR-15 when on a mission."

I walked past Colonel Beck on the way out. He looked over at me. "I understand they have assigned you to one of the better squads. Granted, Psycho and the other members of C4 are all a little on the crazy. They do know how to get results."

I just nodded and walked out without saying a word, carrying that large cardboard box. Just when I started to understand the reality of Vietnam, it changed. A general and captain expressed a desire to see me dead. I am sent to the morgue to get a rifle. There, Lieutenant Doyle gives me a special rifle in a box of body bags. Colonel Beck says I couldn't be attached to a better squad. Could an acid trip be like this?

MISSION ONE PHASE ONE

Fifteen hundred hours came. With our packs on our backs, Psycho had us jog to the airfield, where two UH-1 Hueys were waiting. Several yards away, a Cobra gunship waited to escort us.

Psycho had us so well trained. We knew exactly who got in what Huey and in what order. Once in the air, we headed to the area north of Ben Giang. At the same time, four more Hueys and four more gunships lifted off. They went in the same general direction as us, but when we got close to our LZ, they split off in different directions.

I eventually found out that pretending to land with multiple Hueys and gunships far from the real LZ was a standard procedure. This practice kept the North Vietnamese guessing where we would actually be landing.

Our Hueys hovered a few feet above the ground as we jumped out. Poof, they were gone, along with our gunship escorts. We hiked a hundred yards before securing the area where we would spend the night. I had trouble sleeping. The haunting fear of being overrun by the Viet Cong kept me awake. The sounds of the jungle at night didn't help either.

Somewhere in the night, I fell asleep because the next morning I woke up enjoying the bed I made with green jungle leaves and grass. My eyes remained closed as I tried to separate the distinct smells of the jungle. One smell seemed so out of place. A pleasant sweet herbal fragrance lingered in the air. I turned in the direction of the smell to recognize its source.

My eyes opened to see Shadow sitting on his helmet not five feet from me. His hand was outstretched toward me with a half-smoked joint and a big smile on his face. "Want some?" he asked, offering it to me.

"Nah, maybe later."

Ruben walked over to Shadow and took it from him. After taking a hit, he handed it back to Shadow.

Psycho walked over and kicked the bottom of my feet. "Get up. This is not a time to be lazy and sleep in. Leroy and Sparky are checking the LZ for mines and any other surprises. I need the rest of you lugs to check out our half of the clearing. Be aware there should be another squad checking the other half.

Once that is done, come back and get something to eat. The VIPs and their party should be showing up in a few hours. Once they show up and do their thing, we can be off to do some real work."

I sat up and stashed my gear. Psycho motioned to me. "Stash your gear over there." He pointed to where some camouflage webbing was covering his. "Bring the radio and your rifle. Follow me. I found a good place for us to keep an eye on the day's events."

When we got to where he wanted us to keep an eye on all the activities on the LZ, I started looking around for some dry twigs and grass. Every time I went camping out the next morning, we had a fire and hot coffee.

Psycho glared at me. He came over and kicked my pile of twigs. From the look on his face, I thought he was going to kill me. "This is no fucking camping out. No campfire. Smoke from any campfire gives away our position."

I dropped the twigs I had in my hand. Then I went over to check the radio. I sat quietly, waiting, and hoping not to offend Psycho. I watched for the signal to call Central Command and let them know we were alive and ready to start phase one of our mission.

Psycho positioned us on a rise just outside the clearing. We were able to lie on our stomachs and see the whole LZ. Members of C4 positioned themselves to the left and the right of Psycho and me. When each member of C4 was in position, they could see the LZ and the squad member placed on either side of them. When clear, they could give us a thumbs up.

From across the LZ, the sergeant from Third Squad emerged from the trees on the other side. He gave Psycho the thumbs up. Psycho gave that sergeant the thumbs up back. Psycho looked over at me and nodded.

I got on the radio and keyed the microphone. "This is the Psych Ward, ready to receive our supplies." God, I loved radio code names. It gave radio operators the chance to be creative and funny while making it hard for any Viet Cong listening.

THE BBQ

From the distance, the sound of Huey blades came cutting through the air. I looked up to see the first Huey coming over the treetops. It touched down in the center of the clearing. Three soldiers jumped out. They pulled out a large canvas and folding chairs and tables. The first Huey took off, heading back to base.

A second one touched down just long enough to unload two more soldiers and a fifty-five-gallon drum modified to a barbecue grill. The second one left off and was out of sight.

With amazing precision, a third Huey deposited another four men. They brought with them several cardboard boxes and a big ice chest.

We lay just outside the clearing, watching what followed. The first squad did the setup, which was done with military precision. In a matter of minutes, the LZ turned into an area for an outdoor barbecue with tables and chairs.

I looked at Psycho. "Are they for real? This is a combat zone?"

Psycho looked over at me. "I don't like it either. Remember,

Captain Phillips when you first stepped off the troop transport? Well, this is his catering service."

Psycho filled me in as we watched. "Charlie Company First Squad handled the setup and cooking. Second squad got to be the waiters and entertainment. The third squad was positioned on the other end of the LZ. When Captain Phillips' picnic is over, we get left with cleanup duty. If we are lucky, we will get some leftovers."

The canvas pulled off the first chopper was turned into a tent with two of the sides. Camouflage webbing was thrown over the top. They set three tables under the tent. They placed folding chairs around two of the tables. Soldiers spread white tablecloths over all the tables. The corners were tied with fancy knots.

The grill heated up quickly. Hot dogs and burgers were taken from a cooler and placed on the grill. A small breeze blew in our direction. The smell made me hungry. They placed a large aluminum pot of chili at one end of the grill. My stomach growled. I wanted to go out there and scarf down some of that food.

A soldier went over to the ice chest. He removed the top and lifted a large plastic container. As he removed the lid, my nose caught the aroma of real mustard potato salad. I closed my eyes, wishing I could have some of my mother's potato salad.

"Psych Ward, are you ready for your patients?" Came the voice over the radio. It shocked me back to reality.

I looked at Psycho and said, "Ready."

Psycho looked over at me and nodded.

I keyed the mic and said, "Psych Ward is ready. Bring them on in."

In less than five minutes, a Huey came over the treetops, being escorted by two gunships on either side. The Huey landed about forty feet from the barbecue grill. Waiters and cooks held down items that were light enough to be blown away from the wind created by those Hueys.

The first one to step off was Captain Phillips in perfectly creased Army greens. He looked around. Nodding with approval, he motioned for those in the Huey to come out.

Three gray-haired gentlemen emerged. A moment later, a fourth gentleman who set next to the pilot stepped out of the Huey. He didn't have as much gray hair as the rest. They were all dressed in Army greens with only an American flag patch on their shoulders.

The fourth figure got to where I could see his face. I stopped breathing. Psycho had to poke me with the butt of his rifle butt. The pain got me breathing again. The fourth figure that came off the Huey was General Moorehead.

Psycho grinned. "That's right. It's your General Moorehead. Instead of kissing his mistress, today he is kissing up to any VIP that comes from Washington. He is hoping if he kisses up to the right group, he can get his star back."

I felt sick watching the General and the Captain kiss ass to their guests. I didn't join the Army to give some rich, powerful men the opportunity to have a barbecue in a war zone. From my pack, I pulled out my camera, attached the telephoto lens, and pointed it toward the group. I snapped an entire roll of film, documenting what I saw.

"Are you going to send these photos to the General's wife?" Psycho asked.

"I'm thinking about sending them to a newspaper or two back home."

"You need to wait until all our tours are over. I am afraid of what other hell hole we might get sent to. Since we are here, the only other place left he could send us would be the North Pole. I personally hate the cold."

"Don't worry. I am saving these for a rainy day."

"Good, we have some real work to do in the next part of our mission."

MISSION ONE PHASE TWO

The sun had just set over the treetops when the last of the Hueys carried off Captain Phillips' catering crew. We were glad to see them head back to wherever they came from. We were lucky we didn't have any party crashers from North Vietnam.

Third squad seemed to disappear when it came time to clean up. They were nowhere to be found. We stuffed our packs with what leftovers we wanted and buried the rest.

Psycho reminded us, "It's not safe for us to spend another night near this clearing. All the day's activities is bound to get the attention of some unfriendly patrols. We need to put some distance between us and this clearing."

Psycho pointed at Shadow and then eastward toward Laos. "Take point. Find us a place to spend the night. Make it at least a couple clicks away from here." (A click is equal to one kilometer in distance. A kilometer is just over half of a mile.)

We followed forty feet behind Shadow. It wasn't long before Shadow turned and pointed to Psycho and then to a small clearing off to our left. Psycho had Shadow and Ruben check the area for any unwanted surprises. When they signaled, indicating that the clearing would be where we would spend the night.

C4 had the standard practice of splitting into two groups at night. Each group would camp roughly forty to sixty feet apart. That way, if one camp got attacked, the other camp could come to the rescue of the other. Still, we were not allowed to build any campfires. We ate our rations at jungle temperature.

When we had got settled, Mick pulled out several cans of beer. He passed out a can to each of us.

Psycho gave Mick a glare. "You sneaky bastard. I know they didn't leave us any beer, and I didn't see you sneak down during the picnic."

"They didn't see me either," Mick responded with a grin.

The rest of the squad gave Mick a thumbs up.

"Time to get serious," said Psycho in a low tone. "Remember where we are. We don't know if a VC patrol is close. It's time to do some real work. From here on out hand signals only."

Psycho spoke those words, and I became numb with fear. The most dangerous part of my first mission had begun. The Viet Cong could find our location by any little sound we would make. They could be hiding and waiting for us as we walk past. I had been told they would wait for our guard to be down before attacking.

Psycho made sure I had turned the radio off. That meant it would be hard to get any immediate air or artillery support.

Since I was the newest member of the C4, they gave me the watch from zero two hundred hours to sunrise.

My eyelids kept wanting to close. To stay awake, I started taking everything out of my pack and putting it back. I figured the activity would help me stay awake. While putting everything back, I looked at the climbing rope. It gave me an idea.

As a teenager, I would go deer hunting. My dad taught me how to climb a tree and wait for a deer to come strolling past me. I made a climbing harness from the climbing rope, then I looked around for a tree I could climb.

UP A TREE

I wrapped the rope around the tree and myself. When I reached a good height, I leaned against the rope and put my feet against the tree. 40 feet made a good height to see the surrounding area. From the tree, I could see the area around both of the two C4 groups.

The morning sky took on shades of gray, turning to blue. Out of the corner of my eye, I saw movement. The jungle foliage shifted abnormally. I took aim with my CAR-15 in the direction.

Not knowing what was causing the unnatural movement, I aimed just above where I saw it. I shouted, "Who goes there?" Then fired one round.

"Stop shooting at me!" Mick's head popped up. "Can't a guy take a shit without getting shot at?"

I pointed my rifle in the air. Mick's head went down and popped up again. His sun-tanned face turned almost white. After seeing me up the tree, his face turned red.

A muddy-looking rock flew up from the ground. It arched just enough to hit me on the side of my head. I looked down. Psycho and the rest of the squad were awake and looking up at me. I smiled.

The rifle fire and Mick's screaming rallied the squad. Not knowing what was going on, they came running. All of them prepared for the worst.

Psycho looked up at me. He then glared over at Mick and back at me.

"Get down here!" Psycho barked, pointing to the ground. He gave the rest of the squad the signal to pack up and get ready to move.

I shimmed down the tree expecting a royal chewing out from Psycho. I knew better than to explain my thinking about climbing up that tree. Again, what I thought would be a neat thing got me in trouble with my superiors.

I knew from Psycho's facial expression; I could tell he didn't find my stunt humorous. The members of the squad stood back, waiting. Waiting to see what Psycho would do. I tried hard to read his facial expression, but he stood there poker-faced.

Finally, Psycho spoke, "I am more upset that you did not let any of your squad members know what you were doing.

I am sure Mick didn't enjoy getting shot at while taking a shit."

Psycho motioned the squad to huddle up. He broke one of the many rules while in the jungle.

"I don't want to send any of you home in a body bag. From now on, whoever needs to relieve themselves needs to signal whoever is on guard duty. One finger for going to take a piss, and two fingers for taking a shit. Whoever is on guard duty must respond with the same number of fingers to confirm. Do I make myself clear?"

Everyone responded with a thumbs up.

Then Psycho pulled out a map and set it on the ground in front of all of us. Psycho drew a line with his finger. His finger traced a line east of the Laos border.

"If we were to find any well-traveled trails, I want Mister

Roberts here to take pictures and Sparky to do some of his creative surprises for any VC that comes along."

As we were packing up and ready to move out, Psycho raised his hand in the position that meant stop and pay attention. Then, with his right hand in the air and index finger pointed up, he moved it in a circular motion. We gathered around.

Psycho continued to break his number one rule. While on that first mission, I learned that all of Psycho's rules were subject to change depending on the situation.

"We are going to do something a little different. Our rope-climbing monkey-loving cameraman has taught us a new trick. I know how much you guys love dodging those pits with sharp sticks covered in shit. We can cut our traveling through hazardous parts of the jungle in half."

"Leroy, I want you and our cameraman to go about two hundred yards east and build a Robert's platform."

Hearing Psycho name the platform after me made me feel like I had contributed something to the squad.

"Dave, you stay close to them. If they fall, they are going to need your help. The rest of us will check out where Leroy and Cameraman point us."

Leroy and I looked at each other, smiled, and looked back at Psycho, giving him the thumbs up.

It took Leroy and me a little over an hour to get to where Psycho wanted us and find a suitable tree. It didn't take much time to camouflage our little place up the tree. Leroy took the first watch.

VILLAGE RECON

Leroy and I would move our little tree lookout every day or two. While getting ready to climb my third tree, Psycho motioned for Ruben to swap places with me. Psycho figured I needed more experience on the ground than hanging out in a tree.

Ruben no sooner got settled in the tree when he spotted several huts a couple of clicks away. Psycho's map didn't show a village in that direction. I learned later the North Vietnamese Army disguised their camps as villages. They even brought in women and children to give the appearance of a genuine village.

Psycho, Pham, Mick, Sparky, and I cautiously walked into the village while meticulously examining the ground ahead of us for booby traps. Shadow and Dave stayed behind to guard against any VC approaching. Ruben or Leroy took turns in the tree while the other kept watch from the ground.

Psycho had the five of us stop inside the jungle line, hidden behind the elephant grass. In the clearing, we saw six grass hunts. Psycho had us lie on our bellies and watch the village for two hours. Watching and waiting while at the same time preparing our minds for an attack from the villagers. I never got used to defending myself from a group of angry villagers especially when all they were doing was defending themselves.

We expected to see men, women, and children going about what we considered daily activity. In this village, we saw the women preparing food and doing the laundry. The men pulling weeds in a garden and the children playing. The main reason for the heightened suspicion was the village did not appear on our map.

Psycho explained to me later, he had seen where small villages would move their whole village to escape the war. Because of the war, many of the smaller villages would move themselves and not tell government officials or the VC. They just wanted to be left alone.

The next day, we moved our lookout and camp. The following day, we discovered a somewhat fresh trail coming in from Laos. We followed it away from the border for a couple hundred yards. The trail ended in a clearing where we found four bamboo huts. One hut had a fence made of branches shoved to the ground. No gate, just a break in the fence. Psycho motioned for me to stay while he Mick and Sparky checked out the huts. I didn't see Psycho's signal for me to stay.

I took a few steps toward the hut with the fence. Six feet from the opening, I felt a rifle butt against the back of my head. I swiftly turned and prepared to shoot, then I stopped. There Psycho stood, pointing his rifle at me. I signed, "What up?"

Psycho signed back to me. "You dumb ass! Didn't you see the sign for you to hang back?"

I signed back, "Going to check out this hut."

Fire blazed in Psycho's eyes. He broke one of his rules again. He spoke out loud. "I repeat, you dumb ass. Don't walk through any openings. It could be rigged with a bomb to blow as soon as you walk through it. Now get back!"

I walked away from the fenced hut while keeping my eyes on

it. I cautiously placed one foot behind the other until I was forty feet behind Psycho.

Psycho pointed to Sparky and then to the fenced hut.

Psycho moved back to stand beside me. He motioned for me to kneel. Sparky positioned himself approximately twenty feet from the opening in the fence. He knelt down.

Sparky took a rock a little smaller than the size of a baseball and tossed it through the opening in the fence. It bounced twice, landing close to the entrance of the hut. He took another rock and tossed it. It landed just short of the first one. After the third rock, I thought Psycho and Sparky were being too cautious.

Sparky grabbed a little larger rock. He rolled it toward the opening in the fence. It traveled past the fence opening and headed for the front door of the hut. Halfway to the hut's door when it dropped out of sight. Then BOOM!

The rock shot up out of the hole. It landed on a nearby hut. Flames, along with pieces of the hut and metal, went flying. I kissed the ground and prayed while covering my head. I met with another method if losing my life. Now I feared getting killed from the flying debris.

As the dust settled, Psycho turned to me. "See, you never walk through an opening in a fence or a doorway without first letting Sparky check it out."

I wish I had taken pictures of the before and after of the hut and resulting explosion. Honestly, that explosion set my nerves on edge. I worried if I would make through that day by getting killed from doing something stupid.

NO CAMERA YES GUN

My first impression of Psycho matched his name as the craziest person I ever met. The more time I spent on patrol, I learned Psycho wasn't as crazy as I thought. Psycho had his own unique way of teaching. I must admit, learning through his teaching methods had saved my life so many times.

On every patrol, our number one threat came from the sharpened bamboo sticks covered in shit. We had to keep our eyes peeled for pits covered with leaves. These pits would have a bunch of those sharpened bamboo sticks waiting for us. Or a cluster of them flying at us after crossing a tripwire or stepping on a hidden plate. Those traps kept us on edge and slowed our progress. None of us wanted to endure the pain from the infection that followed.

Before getting shipped off to Vietnam, our instructors warned us about all variations of these traps and how to disarm them. Psycho took our training to the next level. He focused on training our senses. When we were standing down, he would build harmless traps and hide them just outside the base parameter. The next day, he would walk us by where he had set the traps. If we stepped into one of his traps, we would have to do twenty push-ups on the spot. Psycho stressed the value of not stepping into one of his traps. Doing so would increase our chances of losing a limb before our tour of duty was up.

Leroy enjoyed taking his sniper rifle up into a tree. The scope on his rifle allowed him to spot suspicious movement at several hundred yards.

I would relieve Leroy, but I would take my rifle and my camera. On my first mission, I was more focused on taking pictures so the sunrise or sunset. I took some breath-taking scenic photographs.

The day before our extraction, Leroy took the first watch up a tree. Right away, he spotted NVA (North Vietnamese Army) a couple hundred yards out, heading in our direction. Since we weren't going to be making a lot of noise, Psycho deemed it to be relatively safe. I traded places with Leroy to get pictures of them.

I had my eye in the camera's viewfinder when I saw the flash from the barrel of an AK-47. Pieces of the bark flew off from my tree. I screamed down to Psycho, "They're shooting at me!"

"Jump down, we'll provide cover fire," Psycho yelled.

With my camera around my neck and rifle in hand, I jumped down. Shadow softened my fall when I landed on top of him. If it weren't for him, I would have ended up with a broken leg.

As I climbed off of Shadow, I saw him mouth the words, "You're welcome."

Psycho looked at me and tapped his right hip. It meant I needed to position myself by his right side. He had motioned for Mick and Ruben to go wide and flank our attackers. The rest of us hunkered down, keeping them busy with our return fire.

I raised my camera to take a shot. Psycho hit my camera with the butt of his rifle. Knocking it out of my hands. He yelled at me, "Get your rifle and start shooting!"

Frozen with fear, I looked down. My hands were holding a death grip on my camera. Psycho pulled it from my hands. He stared into my eyes and said, "Kill some of those bastards before they get to us or I'm going to shoot you myself."

I grabbed my rifle, aimed at a charging NVA soldier, and fired. That NVA soldier fell to the ground. His buddies kept charging us. Sparky tossed a grenade in their direction. It took out a few more. It only slowed down the rest for a minute.

"How many are there?" I yelled at Psycho.

"You should know, you were up the tree."

"I didn't have time to count."

"Pray we are not getting attracted by more than a small platoon. We don't have the ammo to hold off much more."

Dave came along the left side of Psycho. "We are getting attacked on both flanks. Sparky saw them on his side too."

Dave no sooner than got his words out when Sparky tossed a couple more grenades at our attackers.

Out of the corner of my right eye, I saw this one NVA soldier crawling in our direction.

He saw me, and I looked him in the eye. He stood up to charge me.

I turned and pointed my rifle at him. I fired several rounds right into his midsection. He fell not ten feet from me. A strange sick feeling rose from my gut. I had to turn away and throw up what I had eaten that morning. As hard as I tried, I couldn't hold any of it back.

Psycho looked at me with one of his grins. He mouthed the words, "Your first kill. You did good."

Just as suddenly as it all began, the jungle became silent. Psycho broke the silence with a whistle. It signaled the squad to check in on each other and do a body count.

I looked down at my attacker's corpse. His lifeless eyes made me want to throw up again. I had nothing left in my gut.

Psycho looked over at me. "Are you okay?"

I didn't answer. I stood there shaking.

"Anyone's first up-close kill is a gut wrencher."

I was in such a state of shock, all I could say was, "Yes, yes, sir."

Psycho turned to Dave. "Roberts made his first kill today. He looks like he will need something before he faints. Take care of him."

Dave gave me what he called a happy pill. It took several minutes before my nerves calmed enough to stop shaking.

We didn't bury any of those bodies. Sparky placed the last of his explosives under some of the dead. We rigged their AKs to misfire. This was our way of getting back at the NVA for those bamboo spikes.

We counted sixteen dead North Vietnamese regulars. Mick said he saw a couple running off into the jungle. Psycho didn't want us to go after them because we were running low on ammo.

After eight days trudging through the jungle on my first combat mission, I wanted to climb aboard a Huey and head back to Da Nang. I didn't mind the Huey's shaking and vibrations on the flight back to base. At that point, all I wanted to do is get a warm shower and eat hot food.

DOG PATCH

As soon as our Hueys touched down in Da Nang. A waiting deuce and half truck transported us from the airfield to our hooch. Sergeant Psycho had us trained, even with our return. Psycho and Sparky took our weapons and leftover ammo to lock them away. No one wanted to be that drunk shooting up the base.

The next order of business meant heading for the showers. Living with a week's worth of body odor and dirt doesn't go well in being around other civilized human beings.

After a hot shower and clean fatigues, our third order of business involved food. Not the canned rations or the newer C rations they had started giving to us and the Mac V guys. The mess hall crew delivered roasted chicken, carrots, and onions, fresh baked bread, and apple pie for desert directly to our hooch. The fresh hot food made my body sleepy.

I got little sleep on that first mission. Now all I wanted to do was pass out on my bunk. I had drifted off into dreamland when I felt my bunk shake. I opened my eyes to see Mick shaking it.

"Come on Jason. This is no time to sleep. Time to party."

"Give me a break," I said as I rolled over away from him. "I just want to sleep."

Psycho walked over and gave my bunk a couple of hard kicks. "Put your boots on. It is time for us to introduce you to Dog Patch." Until that day, the only Dog Patch I knew was from the cartoon in the newspaper.

I set up on my bunk and put my boots on. I tried to picture this Dog Patch they talked about. All I could do was chuckle. With Psycho leading the way and Mick behind me, we marched in signal file out the north gate, across the railroad tracks. In the same formation we did when trekking through the jungle. Only this time, we weren't carrying all that gear.

We stayed in that same formation as we walked through the doors of Dog Patch. Immediately, I got hit with the smell of cigarette smoke and fermented booze. I had learned they gave the place the name Dog Patch as a reminder of home. Whoever built it wanted it to be a place where a soldier would feel safe to blow off steam. I must admit, it was the perfect place to blow off steam and decompress from the horrors of war.

According to regulations, Dog Patch was not an approved hangout for U.S. military personnel. Unofficially, Central Command made sure the small huts and its main building were a safe place to unwind. Dog Patch being outside the perimeter of the base, but Central Command made sure patrols included it in their parameter sweeps.

I remember the very first time I stepped into Dog Patch. It reminded me more of a dive bar back home. Cigarette smoke filled the air. The smell of fermented beer mingled with the sweet smell of pot filled the air. Along the right wall a makeshift bar composed of two by twelve planks placed on 55-gallon drums.

Behind the makeshift bar stood a Vietnamese civilian. He had one job. Keep our glasses full. Scattered throughout the room were tables with chairs and wooden makeshift seats. The Rolling Stones' song "In Another Land" played in the background on my first visit.

ONE IN EVERY CROWD

Psycho yelled at the bartender. "A Rookie Round for C4 and double shot for our new guy. Good News! He survived his first mission. I didn't have to shoot him."

The bartender set a shot glass of whiskey and a Mason jar of beer in front of each member of the squad. He set two shot glasses of whiskey in front of me, along with a Mason jar of beer.

Acting as one, we all downed the first shot and rinsed it down with the beer.

Still recovering from the horrible taste of that first shot, Dave slapped me on the back. "Now, down that second shot. You've earned it."

I downed that second one and filled my mouth with beer. I got slaps on the back from each member of the squad and a few that were standing around. After the ceremony, C4 broke off into groups of two or three. They went about reconnecting with other soldiers unwinding from their missions. The effects of the whiskey made me unsteady. I leaned against the bar as a preventive measure from falling over.

While leaning against the makeshift counter, I surveyed the room. Off in one corner, Psycho had joined the other squad leaders. He had the attention of the others as he recited the highlights of our missions.

At one point, Psycho stopped and looked over at me. He motioned for me to join him. When I got close, he pointed to a wooden crate for me to sit next to him. He introduced me to those sitting around the table. They all were team leaders from different Army and Marine recon squads.

"Jason, I want you to tell these guys what you did with the rope and the tree."

I explained how I got bored doing early morning watch. I saw the rope in my pack and thought back to when my dad would take me deer hunting and we would build a platform in a tree. Psycho added, "This is something you should try with your squads. You can recon more area with less risk."

A little later, two MPs entered Dog Patch. They walked past the bar and snaked through the tables. They purposefully made eye contact with different soldiers. The MPs went over and chatted with anyone who looked nervous.

"Don't mind them, kid," said one of the team leaders sitting at my table. "They walk through here occasionally. They look for soldiers who don't report to their duty station."

I felt a set of eyes staring at me from across the room. When I looked in that direction, this big, hairy guy kept staring back at me. At one point, he moved from sitting at a table to standing at the bar.

I tried not to look, but he reminded me more of a grizzly bear with all his black, uncut, unshaved hair. At six feet six, I guessed his weight to be over two hundred and fifty pounds or more. His shirt had the sleeves cut off, revealing hairy arms bigger than my legs.

Three beers later, my bladder screamed for relief. So, I stood up and staggered for the sign that read "Soldiers Relief". I had to walk right past the grizzly, but I had no choice or piss in my pants.

Three feet from the Soldiers Relief, Mister Grizzly stepped in front of me, blocking my path. My eyes went from his chest up to his wild looking eyes. Then I stepped to one side to walk around him. He didn't move. I made it to the pisser just in time.

On the way out, he was standing there waiting for me. He said, "What is a sickly little kid like you doing hanging around with some real men?"

I stood there looking him in the eye while I tried to diffuse the situation. "I am here to just unwind. Let me buy you a beer and we can talk about it."

"I don't want any beer from you. I just want to pound your puny ass into the ground."

From behind me, I heard. "Leave the kid alone."

Out of the corner of my eye, I saw Psycho standing up, along with everyone else at his table. Members of C4 had moved behind me. Mister Grizzly looked past me. Without saying another word, he turned away and walked back to his buddies.

"What's the matter? You are chickening out?" I shouted at Mister Grizzly. "Come on, let's ..." Mick grabbed my right arm and pulled me to the table where he and some others were sitting.

Mick pushed me down in an empty chair. "Listen, Jason, I don't care a lot about the way they run things around here, but who you pick a fight with affects us all. If you picked a fight with that guy, it was obvious you would lose. We all depend upon each other, here and in the jungle. Guys like that one may be an enemy tonight. Sometime down the road, you may need to depend upon him to save your life."

The last thing I remember from that night was playing darts. I had trouble hitting the dart board. They kept falling on the floor.

THE MORNING AFTER

Sometime the next day, I woke up on my bunk with a splitting headache. I moved my head a little. It hurt all the more. I pulled a wool Army blanket over my head to block the sunlight.

The next to my head hurting, I felt a strange pain on my right forearm. When I reached over to touch it, it hurt even more. I opened my eyes to the source of the pain in my arm. All I saw was a blur of red and black. When I finally got my eyes to focus, I saw it. The pain came from my first and only tattoo.

I closed my eyes, thinking I had to be dreaming. Upon opening my eyes again, the tattoo remained. The words of my mother surfaced through the fog of my hangover. "Only those who have been in prison get tattoos" Now when I went home, I had to hide it.

Time passed; my hurting headache eased a little. My eyes still had trouble focusing on my surroundings. I had to squint really hard. After several unsuccessful attempts, I rolled over and pulled the blanket back over my head.

The sun filled the Hooch. With the blanket over my head, I tried to fall back to sleep. Then my brain vibrated from the banging of two trash can lids. I covered my ears. That didn't help.

The banging sound stopped. Then I heard Sergeant Psycho's voice. "It's twelve hundred-hours or high noon for you party animals. You have just enough time to clean up and get some grub in your guts. We have to meet with Captain Phillips for a debrief at zero thirteen hundred hours."

Slowly, I set up. My hangover and the pain on my arm reminded of events I could not remember. The only thing I could do was push through the pain.

Mick walked over to me. "Are you alright, kid?"

"When did I get the tattoo?" I asked.

"You like it?" Mick smiled down at me.

I looked at my arm. Now my eyes allowed me to see more clearly. The faded black lines turned into something recognizable. The letter and number made up C4. Below C4 was a set of crossed bones. Under the crossed bones, the words "Against the Odds".

"Against the Odds", I said, looking up at Mick.

Ruben walked over and stood next to Mick. They both laughed. Their laughter attracted Leroy. He got off his bunk and joined the surrounding group.

Leroy filled me in on what I could not remember. "You were so drunk. You insisted on throwing darts, but you couldn't even hit the dartboard. Out of mercy for you, we dragged you out of Dog Patch."

Dave walked up and picked up from where Leroy left off. "On the way back to the hooch, you passed out. We had to carry you back. When we got back and started talking amongst ourselves. We wanted you to know we accepted you as part of the squad. That's when we decided to formally make you a part of C4.

"Some time back, Pham came up with the design for a tattoo.

So, we put you in your bunk. While you were sleeping, Pham broke out his tattoo kit. That tattoo makes you an official part of C4."

Sparky added. "If you haven't noticed." He displayed his tattoo to me. "Everyone in the squad has the same tattoo." Then the rest of the squad showed me theirs.

"You are now officially part of C4. We all are beating the odds." Mick finished up. "You are here now, and you will be gone when your tour is over. But we don't want you to ever forget we are all on the same shit list. Several high ranking officers would rather see us in body bags than pinning a medal on us. We are doing more than all those soldiers who follow regulation."

I never planned on being part of a combat squad. I just wanted to be a photographer. For some strange reason, that I will never understand. That unforgettable morning, I felt like I belonged.

Psycho stepped between Mick and Dave. "Come on, you cowboys. You've been talking too much. We need to get some chow. Then we got to go over and talk with Captain Phillips."

ROUTINE OF WAR

The rainy season in Vietnam extends from May to early November. It rains in brief bursts, usually in the afternoon. Just long enough for the ground to start to dry out, then it would rain and become mud again.

During those downpours, we would break out our ponchos and find cover until the rain stopped. That is when I discovered the real meaning of Jungle Rot and the necessity of packing multiple pairs of socks.

We would spend a week or more doing recon close to the Laos border. Because we were covered in mud and our maps were smeared with mud, we sometimes couldn't be sure which side of the border we were on. When it came to writing our reports, we said we kept on the eastern side of the border.

Half of our missions involved a fire fights with the North Vietnamese. The other half comprised us fighting mud. If we found a suitable tree, Leroy and his sniper rifle did the recon for us. Then we would investigate any movement he observed.

When we got back to Da Nang, we would hit the showers. During those months, it seemed like after every mission we had the routine of showing to get all the mud we could out of our pores, then off to Dog Patch. On the next afternoon we reported to Captain Phillips. Depending upon his mood, he would either send us back out in the jungle the next day or give us doing some busy work around the base for a week or two. The busy work ranged from emptying the outhouse, hauling base garbage to the dump, or patching holes in the road.

I went to Dog Patch with the guys, because they expected it of me. I dislike having to deal with guys like Mister Grizzly, who thought it was fun to pick on me. As hard as I tried, I could not stay clear of him.

One other regular at Dog Patch made me nervous. The blond-haired sergeant of Captain Phillips liked to stare at me. I recognized him being the sergeant from First Squad and the driver when Captain Phillips met me at Tan Son Nhut. He usually hung out with a group of soldiers from Captain Phillips' catering crew.

This one time, about halfway through the rainy season, we came back from a mission. We fought the mud for the whole week we were out. After spending extra time in the shower, we put on clean uniforms and headed over to Dog Patch. Some mud didn't get washed out of all my hair. I didn't care. I just wanted to get drunk.

We weren't in Dog Patch for thirty minutes before this blond soldier from First squad walked into Dog Patch in a clean and pressed uniform. His boots had a spit shine polished. I downed a couple more shots of whiskey, then staggered over to where this blond guy and his buddies were sitting. I slapped my palms down flat on the table. Looking across the table into the blond sergeant's eyes, I took a deep breath.

"Ya fuck'n poor excuse for being a soldier. You shouldn't be hanging out in a place with real soldiers. Ya should be down at the mess hall and hang out with the pigs that are in the freezer."

The blond sergeant promptly jumped to his feet. I didn't care if he out ranked me or not. I was drunk and intended on whipping his ass.

He looked past me. "Psycho, why don't you come over here and take your boy back to your table?" Psycho had already put his hand on my shoulder. The sergeant continued to talk past me. "Teach him what is really going on in this hellhole. His hummingbird ass is about to get into some real big trouble."

In my left ear, I heard Psycho in a calm voice. "Come on. It is not worth picking a fight with this guy. You may win here, but in the morning you will lose big."

NOT ALL MUD AND BLOOD

When I arrived in Vietnam, General Moorehead gave me an assignment. He wanted me to provide him with combat photos each week via Captain Phillips. After that first mission, Psycho helped me convince the Captain Phillips and the base commander I needed a darkroom to comply with the General's orders.

I ended up sharing a hooch with the ready room for the chopper pilots. The chopper pilots helped me fix up one portion of their hooch as a darkroom. In exchange, I took photos of them so they could send back home. It worked out to be a nice arrangement. It took two months to get all the equipment I needed for that darkroom.

During those two months, Psycho kept telling me, "I will not allow you to stay back so you can work on that darkroom. Your first duty is to support C4 on our missions."

Every couple of weeks, Captain Phillips would come by asking me for some photos to send to the General. When I told him about working on getting the darkroom ready, he would just turn around and walk away. He would come back after the next mission. I would tell him about waiting for the equipment to arrive. Then one day he came asking about the progress of the darkroom. I smiled and handed him a pile of prints from the photos I had taken.

I had to thank Lieutenant Doyle for her help in getting the right chemicals to develop film and the right paper for prints. It turned out I was the only one stationed at Da Nang who snapped and printed their own photographs. Once I had the darkroom up and running, I printed the best of my pictures from C4's missions. I sent copies to General Moorehead and Captain Phillips, while at the same time kept the negatives for myself.

As time went on, I spent time with Lieutenant Doyle. She would have me help her pick up dead bodies that were flown to Da Nang. Sometimes she had me drive her to outlying bases for various errands. Other times she had me take pictures of her with certain backgrounds.

Her official responsibility comprised of preparing the dead before transported back to the states. She would tell me there were times she needed to get out of the morgue. I enjoyed spending time with her.

A few times, Sergeant Psycho accompanied Lieutenant Doyle and me on day trips off to some village. I was told we took those trips because the chopper pilots had complained about no place to land or too dangerous for them. Either way, I got to spend time with Lieutenant Doyle.

Da Nang differed from Tan Son Nhut. Da Nang consisted of Air Force, Marines, Army, and ARVN (Army of the Republic of Vietnam) as well as various civilian contractors. Officially, under the South Vietnamese government's administration. In reality, the United States government ran Da Nang airbase with the South Vietnamese's blessing. With so many groups of people, all with different agendas, made it difficult to get anything accomplished. Those who had their head in the sand labeled Da Nang as a buzzing hub for military operations. I saw it as organized confusion. Either way, it made life easy for Lieutenant Doyle and me to move around with nobody questioning us.

Every Friday, when we were not on a mission, on the way back from the evening mess, a smile came on our faces. We knew a special treat would be waiting for us. In the supply room of our hooch, like magic, appeared two large ice chests. One filled with ice cream and the other Hamm's beer packed in ice.

We knew it came from Lieutenant Doyle. It was her way of expressing her gratitude. She knew if she asked anything of us, we would do it. No questions were to be asked, regardless of the situation.

CHANGE IN THE WIND

I arrived in Vietnam several months after the Tet Offensive in the January 1968. Both US and South Vietnamese installations saw a coordinated attack. After the defeat of the North Vietnamese and Viet Cong forces, a false sense of security remained. That false security got shattered on the morning of August 23rd, 1968. Anyone sleeping that morning got awakened to a large amount of small arms fire and explosions. We jumped from our bunks and ran to the weapons closet. Psycho passed out our rifles and extra clips of ammo. Only after leaving the hooch did, we realize that the gunfire originated from Central Command North.

The building that housed Central Command North, along with other administrative buildings and several barracks, was a short distance from the bay. No one expected an early morning attack from the water.

At roughly three o'clock on the morning of August 23rd, over a hundred North Vietnamese Army special forces came ashore. Most of them were wearing just shorts and carrying AK-47s. A few carried belts with grenades attached. They were clearly on a suicide mission.

Central Command North had standing orders for regular overnight patrols. If it weren't for those patrols, the death toll would of have been much higher. We only lost sixty American soldiers and forty-eight wounded.

Our hooch was at the far western end of the airfield. Until that morning, the powers that be expected that if Da Nang got attacked, the attack would come from the west. Since they classified C4 as an expendable squad, we would be the first to get hit. Not so, that morning of August 23rd.

As we ran toward the sound of automatic weapon fire, a Marine Colonel intercepted us. He pointed out we only had on our underwear and told us to stand down and said if we went there shooting in the dark, we could be mistaken as the enemy. He ordered us to stand outside our hooch and wait.

As the sun came up over the South China Sea. The sound of gunfire dissipated, all but for an occasional burst from an M16.

When they released us, the fighting was over. We were left with the task of separating dead NVA from their weapons. We had to create a pile for the dead NVA. Another squad got the task of digging a mass grave for them. We had the duty of separating ammo from weapons and storing them. Other units took care of our wounded, while Lieutenant Doyle oversaw our dead.

From the months that followed, no one could relax while at Da Nang. Even the sound of a backfiring truck sent soldiers running for cover. Rumors were going around about the North Vietnamese Army and the Viet Cong only were testing waters for another invasion. We feared another Tet Offensive, or worse, would happen soon.

November finally came. The rainy season ended. The North Vietnamese would have an easier time moving troops and supplies. This meant our down time turned into more time in the jungle. We went from seven days to fourteen days, sometimes longer.

It also meant we could also move through the jungle without letting our presence being known. Our orders went from strict recon to giving them as much hell as we could.

At home, we heard things were getting chaotic. Tricky Dick Nixon got elected President. On college campuses, protesters were calling for us to leave Vietnam. The Black Power movement had white folks worried.

Things weren't much better in Nam. South of us, we heard a rumor of a platoon had killed five hundred Vietnamese friendlies. Lieutenant Doyle told me General Moorehead had started running a protection racket on businesses in Saigon. She also found out Captain Phillips and General Moorehead were related. Psycho got word that Captain Phillips doctored our field reports. Our reports now read as reports from the first squad. The Captain still ran his catering service.

At one of Captain Phillip's outings, a VC sniper put a bullet through a senator's can of beer. This forced the Captain to look for a safer location to have his outing.

One morning, after getting back from a week-long trek in the jungle, we received some interesting news about one of the base's barbers. He was a local Vietnamese. During the day, he would cut soldiers' hair. At night he would sneak outside the base parameter and shoot at American soldiers on patrol. One patrol shot back and killed him.

As a squad, we stopped going to Dog Patch. We feared a grenade would get tossed through a window or the door. Pham went a couple times to check it out. The more daring squads were still going. They would have a couple of their own pull guard duty outside, while the rest would party.

Those who patrolled were getting jumpy. Twice, a patrol saw

a blade of grass move in a breeze, they would get cut down with several bursts from a M16.

LT DOYLE AND ME

From my time in Germany and with Psycho, I learned not to ask questions. I would just say, "Yes sir," and follow orders. I knew that Lieutenant Alice Carson Doyle had to be more than just an army nurse. Like the time Psycho sent me to see her for my rifle and the trips we would take to outlining villages. While on those trips, she would have me take photographs of her. When we would get back to base, she would have me print them out and give them to her with no explanation.

This one day, Lieutenant Doyle and I had just got back from one of her errands. She had set some papers on her desk. I finally mustered the courage to ask her, "Why are you always having me take photographs of you like the one you repeatedly have me take on that street corner in Hoi An?"

Until that afternoon, she would give orders and directions. Our conversations centered on a mission C4 had come off or what I could do to be a better asset to her and C4. So, asking Lieutenant Doyle about something she didn't volunteer took a lot of courage on my part.

Without saying a word, she got up and walked over to the filing cabinet and pulled out two photos I had previously taken.

She placed them side by side on her desk. She asked, "Can you tell me what the differences are between the two photos?"

At first glance, they appeared to be two identical photos. She was wearing her Army greens, standing next to a wooden pole. On Doyle's head was the traditional Vietnamese cone-shaped straw hat she liked to wear. Behind her, and across the street, stood a man in the doorway of a shop.

"I don't see any difference. What am I looking for?" I asked.

"Take a closer look at the shopkeeper in the left photo and then at the shopkeeper in the right photo. What is the difference?"

I put my face closer to each photo. "In the right photograph, the man is wearing a flowery shirt. On the left photograph, he is wearing a solid-colored shirt."

"Good. I knew you couldn't be totally blind." I normally would write off her sarcastic comments as being her an officer talking to an enlisted man. That day, the tone in her voice was different.

"So, what is so important about him wearing two different shirts? Other than me taking them on two different days."

"The shopkeeper wore the flowery shirt, telling me he had spotted NVA troops near his village. The solid color shirt told me he had seen none."

"So he is a spy warning you? What do you do with that information?"

"I pass it on up the chain of command."

She motioned me to follow over to an adjoining room where several wooden caskets with dead soldiers were waiting for transport back to the states. "I know you must have a lot of questions about what I do here, but it is in your best interest to just follow orders and let me worry about the why."

"Yes, ma'am."

"What I can tell you is we have several informants who don't want to go through official channels. I am tasked with covertly gathering intel from them and passing it on. Because of my relationship with those sources, I can help you and C4 at the same time."

After that day, our conversation during those errands and at the morgue changed. I felt she trusted me more. She told me how she would push the boundaries of regulations to accomplish what needed to be done. I didn't always feel good about what she did. I convinced myself it was for the greater good.

Something changed between the two of us. She would talk about the trouble she had growing up in San Francisco with a Japanese mother and a Caucasian father. She had to keep secret her father working for the police department and her uncle for the FBI. I didn't know how to take it when she told me about getting drafted by Army intelligence, after college.

I even shared my life's story with Lieutenant Doyle. I told her about growing up in Idaho. In summer, the family camping trips. The weekend hunting trips in the back country with my uncle and dad. She couldn't believe in a rural place like Idaho I could go fishing in the Summer, hunting in the fall, and skiing in the winter. Before she met me, she thought everyone in Idaho worked on a potato farm.

Lieutenant Doyle understood my preference to shooting with a camera over shooting with a gun. I heard her say several times, "You can do more good or bad with a camera. A gun is only good for killing."

FIELD PROMOTION

The first week of November was when it happened. We left the mess hall after eating breakfast. Psycho told us to go on to the Hooch. He said he needed to see our platoon's clerk and perhaps visit them at Central Command North. I didn't think much about what he said. We were due to head out on another mission.

Psycho took an unusually long time to get back to the Hooch. The guys in the squad acted strange. That got me nervous. After going through life and death situation with the same bunch of guys, everyone developed a sense what each other is feeling.

Psycho entered our hooch around eleven hundred hours. He motioned for us all to meet out back and gather around our makeshift picnic table. I expected a briefing for our next mission.

Sergeant Psycho held a large vanilla envelope. "Corporal Jason Roberts," he ordered, staring directly at me. "Stand up and stand right here," He pointed to a spot next to where he was standing.

"Yes, sir." I stood next to Psycho. I dreaded I had done something drastically wrong. Psycho did not have the habit of calling anyone of us out when gathered like that.

He pulled a sheet of paper from the vanilla envelope. Psycho continued. "Since they assigned you to us. Over the past few months, you have proven yourself better than any of us had hoped. Despite being a combat photographer in the US Army, fighting beside you has been a pleasure."

Psycho placed the paper on the table. "I need you to sign this."

Dave handed me a pen. "Don't read it, just sign on the dotted line."

"What is this for?" I looked down at the paper. My eyes caught the words Sergeant Jason Roberts at the bottom of the paper.

"What is this?"

"Just sign it. I hope you have learned to trust us by now." Mick said.

Psycho tapped his index finger on where I was to sign. "It has taken a lot of work to get this. Colonel Beck, Lieutenant Doyle, and all of C4 worked together to pull in some mighty powerful favors. You are being given a field promotion from Corporal Jason Roberts to Sergeant Jason Roberts in the United States Army."

Psycho reached back into the envelope and pulled out the little gold pieces of cloth with the sergeant chevron.

I just stood there, speechless. Not knowing whether to be happy or sad. I didn't expect or want a promotion. My only desire was to get back home in one piece. Then my ears got filled with congratulation and slaps on my back. When the congratulations were over, I mustered enough internal fortitude to look up from the ground and at the guys. Everyone stood up and snapped to attention. All of C4 saluted me as one unit. I humbly returned their salute.

I bent over and signed the paper. Then I turned back around.

I saluted Psycho. He returned mine. "You are now officially second in command of this squad."

I saluted Sergeant Psycho again.

I started to sit down when I heard Psycho. "Just a minute, we have one more item." he put his hand up to get everyone's attention. Everyone got quiet. Their faces turned to a sober look.

"What else is there?" I thought to myself.

"Sergeant Roberts, get the squad ready. We are to board two UH-1B's in one hour. We caught a short mission. The mission will only last for three days."

I turned and looked at the squad. "Gear up! Plan for a four-day mission."

I turned back to Psycho and asked, "Do I still carry the radio?"

"Yes, you still carry the radio, along with your extra responsibilities."

In less than an hour, I had become a rookie corporal looking to just stay alive. To my surprise, a promotion. I now shared the responsibility of the whole squad. I felt like the weight of responsibility on my shoulders had more than doubled. Before I just carried the radio. Now every man's life rested on mine and Psycho's shoulders. I could no longer allow myself the luxury of making mistakes. If I made any mistakes, it could cost the lives of one or all of C4. All my decisions had to be right.

A FIRE FIGHT

Two days out looking for any foot paths coming off from the Ho Chi Minh trail. We had got word somewhere in our patrol area, supplies were getting to NVA units south of us. The brass wanted the supply route found and found like yesterday.

A lot of NVA's supply routes were too narrow for a truck or motor vehicle. This meant we had to keep our eyes out for weighted bicycle tracks or a group of footprints. We plowed through the trees and foliage looking for well-worn trails. When we did, Sparky would go to work setting explosives for the next caravan of supplies.

We feared if we came across one of these supply caravans, it would be an ambush. Other squads were not as lucky as us. We heard of a whole LRRP (Long Range Recon Patrol) squad getting ambushed and wiped out. Every member of C4 constantly asked themself, "What are we not seeing?" "Which one of us is going to take a bullet or, worse, get killed?"

We started getting in at least one firefight each time out. The tension and fatigue from making our own paths through the jungle added to the exhaustion. Our eyes and ears strained to catch anything out of place.

We had entered a little depression between two hills. Without warning, the popping sounds of an Ak-47 echoed around us. We ran for cover. Bullets flew overhead.

We could see the flash of rifle fire coming from the rise fifty yards on our left. They greatly outnumbered us. Every man took cover and started firing back at them. I turned on the radio and checked our coordinates.

Psycho looked at me. He gave me a nod and a hand signal.

I keyed the mic. "Psychic Ward in need of air support. We're taking heavy fire." We were usually in a place where air support was not available. That day, we were lucky.

"What is your position?"

I pulled out the map. After noting our position and our attacker's location, I radio their position.

I heard it over the radio. "We have a couple of sharks heading your direction. They will be there in five." Sharks, slang for helicopter gunship.

Bullets flew past our heads. Every attempt to advance on our attackers failed. Those five minutes got longer when our ammo supply noticeably declined. None of us wanted to run out of ammo before the sharks arrived. It meant we would lose; our knives to their guns.

We stopped returning their fire. We waited and listened until they stopped. If we saw anyone stand up or head our direction, then one of us would take them out. This technique saved us ammo and kept them from overrunning our position.

The Sharks finally showed up. I radioed confirmation where we wanted them to strike. I tossed a can of yellow smoke to mark our position. I didn't want us getting hit by their machine gun fire when they were supposed to be helping us.

After the second run from the gunships, things got quiet. The

Sharks left. To get a better position, Shadow jumped up and ran to hide behind a tree. Out of nowhere a bullet hit Shadow's upper leg. One of our attackers was still alive. Sparky tossed a grenade at him. We did hear from him again. Dave, seeing what happened, ran over to bandage his wound.

About the same time, Leroy saw a grenade flying in the air toward him. He jumped out of the way a little bit too late. The blast caught Leroy midair and propelled him another twenty feet before he landed. Leroy almost landed on top of me. I could tell he looked quite rattled. Not knowing if he had any internal injuries from the blast. I motioned for Dave to check Leroy out.

I didn't wait for Psycho's signal. I keyed the radio mic again. "This is the psych ward. We need an immediate dust-off and EVAC." Dust Off was radio jargon for a medivac chopper. EVAC stood for "Get us the hell out of here."

When we thought the firefight was over we came under attack from a stronger wave than before. A wide pattern of bullets were coming in our direction. There must of have been at least a hundred of them and only nine of us.

Over the radio came the words no soldier wants to hear: "No medivac or EVAC is available. Your LZ is too hot. Cool it down before we can help you." I didn't want to relay the bad news on to Psycho or any of the guys.

The gunships significantly reduced the number of enemies shooting at us. They gave us some breathing space. Psycho was able to make sure everyone else was okay. He checked on how much ammo we had left.

I didn't notice Mick and Ruben were sneaking on both flanks of our attackers. Sparky positions himself with a pile of grenades.

Dave had dragged Shadow back behind where I was positioned. Dave had put a field dressing on Shadow's wound and gave him some morphine. Then he came over to check on

Leroy. Leroy has set himself up against a tree. He kept blinking his eyes like he was trying to focus.

Sparky started pulling pins and lopping grenades at our attackers as fast as he could. Ruben and Mick picked up some of the enemies AKs and started using their own weapons against them. Psycho and Pham did the same. I stayed back to cover Dave and our wounded.

WAITING

The sound of gunfire and explosions ceased. An eerie silence filled the jungle again. We waited. The smoke from Sparky's exploding grenades cleared. Psycho gave me the hand signal to call for choppers.

"Psychic Ward to North Star, Things have cooled down. We are ready for Dust Off and EVAC."

"Choppers are busy. It will be at least one hour." My heart sunk to my gut. The enemy could get reinforcements and overrun us within an hour.

I hesitantly relayed the news over the Psycho. As a squad, we held off our attackers. Now we had to wait some more. Psycho motioned for me to regroup everyone where Dave was attending to Shadow and Leroy.

Psycho broke one of his rules and gave us verbal orders. "We are going to be here for a while. Mick, you, Ruben, and Pham get a body count. Make sure they are all dead. We don't want any of them playing dead and coming back to life and then bite us in the ass. Then gather up what weapons and ammo we can use."

Psycho turned to me. "I want you to help Sparky put together some of his creative work for anyone else who comes through here. Wait until Mick's team gets finished, I want to leave as many surprises as we can. The rest of us will provide cover fire for any unwelcome visitors."

Everyone got their assignments finished before any NVA showed up. We changed our EVAC site up a hill about a hundred yards away. I helped Dave drag Shadow up the hill. Mick watched Leroy because he still looked a little unsure of himself.

We waited another two hours before a UH-1B and UH-1C Hueys showed up. The UH-1C Huey had a red cross and racks for stretches, while the UH-1B Huey was set up for troop transport.

Back in Da Nang, medics sent Shadow to the base hospital. On his second day there, Shadow informed the doctors and nurses he no longer needed their services. He stood up and hobbled across the base to our hooch. None of the nurses or orderlies dared to stop him.

The doctors wanted to keep Leroy for two days, just to make sure he didn't have any permanent damage to his brain from the grenade blast. After all, it only threw him twenty feet or more. After two days, the doctors cleared Leroy for duty, but he wanted to stay longer. He met this pretty nurse. They spent a lot of time flirting with each other.

While Shadow and Leroy were in the hospital, we were on stand-down status. During that time, they had us do cleaning and maintenance around the base. Twice we did night patrol with the black ops guys on the parameter. I got to spend more time with Lieutenant Doyle.

I didn't wait for a request from Lieutenant Doyle. After breakfast, I would head straight over to the morgue. She always had something where she needed my help. I usually finished helping her about the time the sun went down. She always had me carry something back to C4's hooch. It usually comprised a bag of what she called treats for the guys. Most of the time, the bag contained our special bullets and sometimes explosives for Sparky. She called it her way of thanking C4 for letting me help her.

I knew the Mac V operators would hand load their ammo. They had a certain combination of gunpowder and a certain weight of lead. It gave better results than regular Army issue. Although C4 had the classification of Long-Range Recon Patrol, plus being the shit list of General Moorehead made is difficult getting decent ammo.

I found out through Lieutenant Doyle had a way of convincing the Mac V operators to set aside some much of their special ammo for her each week. She would pass that ammo on to C4.

She even had a source to get us claymores with electric and non-electronic triggers. Sparky loved that. He got excited when Lieutenant Doyle gave me plastic explosives and pressure-sensitive detonators for him.

Regardless, I enjoyed spending time with Lieutenant Alice Doyle. I would walk into the morgue. She would look up at me and shoot me a welcoming smile. From time to time, I would escort her on errands to various places on base. If we were to be off base during lunch hour, she would pack us sandwiches and soda pop. I didn't mind cleaning the toilets in the morgue. The regulation about officers and enlisted men be damned. We enjoyed spending time with each other.

BAD NEWS FOR THE HOLIDAYS

My only Thanksgiving Day in Vietnam was not anywhere like the Thanksgivings I spent back home. In Idaho, my family would gather around this expanded dining room table. The smell of cooked turkey and pumpkin pie filled the air. My Thanksgiving in Germany comprised turkey, dressing, mashed potatoes, and all the trimming served by some visiting movie stars and a politician. It helped make me feel appreciated.

The heat and humidity in Vietnam didn't feel like the Thanksgiving Day I ever experienced. The only resemblance of the day was when we visited the mess hall. They served turkey with all the trimmings. We were thankful for the food and breathing.

That morning, Psycho came back from Central Command North with orders for our next mission. We were to leave the following day. To keep us busy, Psycho sent us to the firing range. After the squad just got back, Psycho filled the squad in on the mission details. The rest of the day, we spent cleaning our weapons. We packed enough ammo and food for a week.

The sun had just gone down. Out of the corner of my eye, I noticed Sergeant Psycho standing in the doorway, staring at us. I couldn't make out the shadowy figure who was standing behind him.

"Attention shun!" Psycho shouted. Everyone jumped to their feet and stood in front of our bunks. We all thought some officer had come by for a surprise inspection. C4 rarely got inspected by the brass or by some visiting official.

Sergeant Psycho stepped forward into the room. Lieutenant Alice Doyle stepped from behind him and to his right. It was one of the few times I saw her dressed in full uniform with patches. That was the first and only time I ever saw her visit our hooch.

When we were all in position, eyes facing forward, Sergeant Psycho said, "As you were." Psycho and Doyle moved to the middle of the room. "The Lieutenant is here because she has something very important to tell you. She asked me to tell you in person. Now, I want you to know, what she has to tell us is purely off the record."

Lieutenant Doyle motioned with her hands and said, "Gather around. There is no need for anyone else to hear."

She scanned each one of our faces. "Get closer. I don't bite." We closed in tighter around her. Psycho stayed next to her.

"As you know, if not suspected, I have been able to supply you with top-notch weapons and ammunition used by the MAC V operators. I regret to inform you, my source has been cut off."

Each member of the squad shot a fearful glance at each other. Our hearts fell. What we got from Lieutenant Doyle was the edge that made us so successful. Now our tough assignments just got tougher and more dangerous.

Doyle cleared her throat. "I won't be able to get you anymore for some time. Your modified CAR-15 will shoot the same nine-millimeter rounds the North Vietnamese Army uses. You will have to take the ammunition off the NVA you kill. As far as gun oil and replacement parts for your CAR-15s. I recommend, when you run out, have an AK-47 ready. I don't know if you will get replacements through regular supply channels. Any questions?"

We didn't know what to say. I believe every one of us was thinking the same thing. "Just when life was getting a little easier or better, something comes along and ruins it."

I asked, "Will you ever be able to supply us again?"

Doyle gave me the same look I would get when my mother would give me when my dad said no and I would go to her to get her permission. She would give this look and tell me, "Sorry, I can't. Your father has spoken."

A sad Lieutenant Alice Doyle took a deep breath. She turned away and walked out.

We started talking amongst ourselves. Psycho raised his hand for us to be quiet. "I know this is the last thing you want to hear from me. Especially the day before going on a mission. If we are careful and play it smart, we just might have enough ammo for our next mission. Be prepared to collect all AK ammo you can carry. We are going to need all we can get."

SOMETHING NOT RIGHT

This time a truck took us from our hooch to two waiting UH-1B Hueys. We usually walked. The Hueys flew further south than our regular patrol area. They dropped us off in the northern portion of what we knew as the Iron Triangle. No longer in NVA territory. Now we had to watch out for signs of NVA and Viet Cong. In this area, many villagers sympathized with the Viet Cong.

We were in the same area where two years ago Operation Cedar Falls failed. Back then the Army brass believed since the Viet Cong lacked the same level of training as the North Vietnamese soldiers, the Army could clear the area of the Viet Cong. Not so. The Cong excelled in hiding and outmaneuvering the US forces.

I could tell from the look on each team member's face. All of us were worried that we would be the next squad that would get ambushed and wiped out. No one said a word. If someone had said something, that would have lessened our chances of getting out alive. Psycho kept us moving forward like all the previous missions.

We had trouble understanding why Captain Phillips chose

this particular clearing for his next barbecue. No one in C4 liked Captain Phillips. He had one goal while in South Vietnam. He wanted to impress all politicians and ranking officers, so when his tour of duty was over, he would get a plush job back stateside.

On his last barbecue further north, a senator got a beer shot out of his hand by a sniper. Captain Phillips moved this barbecue closer to Saigon.

Everyone in the squad waited for the day we could get back at Captain Phillips for making us suffer through the smell of hamburger cooking and beer, then having to clean up their mess.

Psycho warned us. "We need to be on extra alert. The Viet Cong could be watching us. We just might see an attack while the captain's barbecue is in progress."

If we were lucky, the captain's barbecue would go off without any problems. We hunkered down just inside the tree line. This time Psycho positioned half of us facing inward, watching the Captain's party. The other half lay facing outward, watching for any unusual movement.

The next morning, we woke up and ate our cold rations. Psycho made sure we had spread ourselves ten feet apart. We waited for when the Hueys would show up to get everything ready for the Captain and his guest.

I sat ten feet to the right of Psycho; I saw some of the tall grass move in the morning breeze. Psycho glanced over at me. "I need to check something out."

He stood up and carefully stepped toward the center of the clearing. I strained to see what got Psycho's attention. The only movement I saw came from the grass moving in the breeze. It didn't seem strange.

Psycho looked in my direction again. He tilted his head toward the center of the clearing. Something inside me said I should stop him. I had trouble describing the turmoil I felt in my gut. I wanted to say something to Psycho, but I knew better. He should've sent me to investigate the movement.

I couldn't figure out why Psycho moved his head and his rifle from left to right as he walked to the center of the clearing. Then he pointed toward something. I raised my rifle to provide cover for him.

IT'S WRONG

Psycho fired three rounds straight at the ground a few feet in front of him. I saw a mist of red flying up in the air. Two figures wearing black pajamas popped up and charged Psycho. I saw repeated muzzle flashes coming from their weapons.

Psycho pointed his rifle at them and sent a spray of bullets, causing them to fall. Psycho just stood there, firing at the other end of the clearing. The next minute, he dropped out of sight.

The two more black pajamas raised up, letting loose with full auto in our direction. From the other side of the clearing, several more emerged wearing black pajamas running in our direction. Bullets flew past Psycho like they knew where we were.

I was told later that the Viet Cong had taken out all of Third Squad. Some of them were sneaking into positing in the center of the clearing when Psycho got curious. They must have been waiting for Captain Phillips's catering service to show up and then ambush them.

A shower of rounds from AK-47s flew at us. Leroy, Mick, and Sparky returned fire. Over the sound of gunfire, I heard nothing from Psycho. At that point, I couldn't see him either. I immediately realized that we were outgunned and needed help.

I rolled on my back, checked our coordinates on the map, and keyed the mic. "This is Psych Ward. We are in need of an immediate fire sale!"

Not waiting for an answer, I turned back over and grabbed my CAR-15, sending off a couple of bursts. I waited for Psycho to show up on my left side. He didn't show. I didn't see any movement near where I saw him fall. At that point, I had to act without Psycho, or all of us would be dead.

To my right, I saw two more Viet Cong running toward us. I raised my rifle and took them out like ducks in a shooting gallery.

I signaled the squad by raising my middle finger in the air. It signaled to everyone we were fucked and need to fall back and regroup. Just in case any of the guys didn't see my signal, I screamed above the gunfire. "Fall back! Fall Back! And regroup!"

Shadow stood up to run. He fell flat on his face. Dave crawled in his direction.

The rest of the squad moved back in a leapfrog pattern until we regrouped a hundred feet back.

I attempted to move forward to help Psycho. The charging VC and gunfire prevented me. Ruben told me later he saw the VC dragging off Psycho's body.

Sparky started tossing grenades at our attackers. Pham took out one who tried to sneak up on our left side. Leroy moved back to a rise, where he picked off attackers with his sniper rifle.

Shadow got hit a couple more times when he tried to stand up. Dave helped him get to the rear. Mick and the rest provided cover fire so we could get regrouped.

My fear of getting killed, or worse, looked real.

EVAC TIME

Just as quickly as all hell broke loose, with bullets flying past, an eerie silence filled the jungle. We waited for more sounds of AKs firing at us. Psycho had spoiled the VC's plans. Dave gave all the medical attention he could to Shadow, but he definitely needed more. I wasn't sure how much ammo we still had left. For us to survive, we needed to get out of there, quickly.

I got on the radio. "This is Cameraman. The Psych Ward needs EVAC! The crazies are coming at us. We need air support fast! We have one, maybe two in need of a Dust Off." I knew about Shadow. I kept hoping to see a wounded Psycho running as us while being chased.

I waited. And waited. Instead of news over the radio, I heard the screams of the charging Viet Cong. I felt bullets flying past me again.

"Return selected fire!" I screamed. "Make sure every bullet counts."

Over the sound of war, I heard from the radio. "This is CCN. Contain those crazies. Repeat contain those crazies or we can't EVAC you." CCN stood for Command-and-Control North.

I recognized the voice on the other end. The one captain's voice in all of Vietnam I didn't want to hear came over the radio. I always felt Captain Phillips wanted to see all of C4 killed in action. By not sending any help confirmed it.

I keyed the mic again. "Too many crazies. Repeat too many crazies. We have wounded, possibly one KIA (Killed in Action). Send help! We need Dust Off and EVAC at the secondary location."

Over the last several missions, Psycho and I had arranged with Central Command to plan alternate EVAC locations. We did this so we wouldn't waste time on the radio or give the enemy our EVAC locations. Primary and secondary EVAC locations were usually clearing or hilltops a couple of miles from each other. We heard rumors the VC would listen to our radio transmissions. To confuse the VC, our EVAC locations were given names like Alpha 1 or Beta 1. Denoting primary and secondary EVAC locations

"Where is Psycho?" I screamed. "Has anyone seen Psycho?"

Dave and Ruben both pointed to where they last saw him. That's where I saw him fall. My heart sank. The attacking Viet Cong was now between us and where I saw Psycho fall.

The overpowering number of VCs prevented us from successfully grabbing Psycho's body. Since all of us had a bounty on our heads: dead or alive. Those VCs would have loved to cash in on the bounty of us all.

Dave tapped on my shoulder. I turned to see the fear in his eyes. "If any of us are going to get out of here alive. You are going to have to forget about Psycho and take charge. Now get us out of here!"

"No time to mourn," I thought to myself. All the training and coaching Psycho and Lieutenant Doyle had done kicked in. I motioned for the squad to move to our secondary extraction point at the top of the hill behind us. We could make our stand until the Hueys arrived.

Leroy was the first to reach the hilltop. He positioned himself so he could pick off any of the VCs following us. Dave and Pham were under each of Shadow's arms. They were dragging him up the hill. Sparky took up the rear. He laid down some of his quick mines. Once everyone was at the top of the hill, we positioned ourselves defensively.

I felt something bounce off my helmet. It knocked my head sideways. It turned out one of those flying bullets kissed my helmet. I hated wearing those metal helmets in the jungle's heat. After that day, I made sure I wore it.

It seemed like an eternity before we heard a couple of gunships coming over the treetops toward us. I directed the squad to where I wanted to put down covering fire. We waited. Still, no medevac chopper or any Hueys for us to jump into.

"I'm out of ammo," I yelled. Then I looked down to see my camera hanging from my neck. I set my rifle down and snapped several pictures of our last day. If we were all going to die, I wanted to have some record of C4's last stand. I always wondered if General Custer would have taken pictures if he had a camera. I snapped shots of each member, thinking inside we were only moments from our end.

On my right, I eyed a VC sneaking up on me. I remembered the Browning HP in my shoulder holster. I pulled it out. The same one Psycho gave me when I first got to Nam. I always counted it as a sort of good luck charm.

I placed two nine-millimeter slugs in the forehead of that sneaking bastard. He fell six feet from me. With my other hand, I reached around behind me and pulled the mic from the radio.

"This is Cameraman. Where are those Hueys?" I only heard static from the radio. I placed two more nine-millimeter slugs in the chest of another attacker. That VC climbed over the dead body of his buddy. I put a third one on the forehead of another.

Finally, I heard multiple sets of chopper blades. I looked eastward. Two gunships escorting a Choctaw UH-34C headed our way.

REGROUPING

They sent Choctaw UH-34C for our extraction instead of our usual UH-1B Huey. The Choctaw UH-34C carried all of us. Known for being larger and faster than the utility helicopters. It had only a range of 170 miles. That meant we had to stop and refuel at least once before reaching Da Nang.

The two gunships sprayed our attacker's position. Those VCs turned from being aggressors to fleeing chickens looking to stay alive. The gunships gave us enough time to board our ride. Once in the air, I checked on the condition of each squad member.

I noticed Mick was sitting on one butt cheek. "Hey, Mick, are you okay?"

"I'm okay, just a rough one." He waved me off.

"Are you sure? You are sitting kinda funny."

"I caught one in my right butt cheek," Mick responded while looking away.

"You could have been shot in worse places," I said with a smile.

Ruben looked dazed. I called out his name. Ruben just sat there looking past me. I motioned for Dave to go over and check him out.

Dave discovered blood rolling down behind Ruben's left ear. After taking off Ruben's helmet, Dave discovered a bullet went up inside Reuben's helmet. It tore some of his scalp. Dave applied a field dressing over it.

The chopper touched down on the helipad next to a field hospital. We left Shadow, Ruben, and Mick for medical attention. A few minutes later, the chopper crew refueled and took the rest of us back to Da Nang.

I stepped out the side door of the UH-34C. I saw a jeep heading toward us. In the passenger seat was our beloved Captain Phillips. The jeep stopped twenty feet from us.

All worn out, we didn't want to give the Captain our full attention or salute. Our salutes looked more like a halfhearted wave.

The Captain climbed out of his Jeep and walked over to us. The smell of our body odor caused him to take four steps back. He couldn't say much. We just came from a few days of hell.

"I see a North Vietnamese soldier gets to claim the bounty for Psycho." Captain Phillips punctuated his statement with an evil grin. "Well, that makes one less headache for me."

"They were VC, sir," I said correcting the Captain.

Lucky for the Captain, he stood out of arm's reach. Otherwise, I would have decked the SOB on the spot. But that would not have done me or C4 any good. Instead, I took note as to the kind of karma I wanted to inflict on him down the road. Right now, we needed showers, food, and to head back out to get Psycho's body.

It didn't take any genius that General Moorehead was the only one who could have ordered the delay in our EVAC. From my arrival, General Moorehead informed me that he intended to see me go home in a body bag. I suspect Captain Phillips had us patrol in a strange area so we could get ambushed.

The past twenty-four hours confirmed, our biggest threat

came not from the Viet Cong or the North Vietnamese Army, but from General Moorehead and Captain Phillips. We were allowed to shoot the VC and NVA, but General Moorehead and Captain Phillips were off-limits.

After hitting the showers, we headed for the mess hall for some hot food. Then on to Dog Patch to get drunk. We had survived an attack from over a hundred enemy soldiers. The idea of one of them throwing a grenade into Dog Patch was the least of our worries. We just wanted to get drunk.

Standing at the bar, I looked over at the table where Psycho usually set. It set empty. That empty chair was a reminder. Tomorrow, we need to go back and retrieve Psycho's body.

Later that night, Pham, Dave, and Leroy were still partying strong. I staggered out of Dog Patch. The booze wasn't helping the anger and sense of helplessness I felt. A long walk in the hot humid night air did little to help me forget the pain I felt in my gut. A couple of soldiers on guard duty offered their condolences for losing Psycho. I walked past them without saying a word.

Before I left Dog Patch, a squad leader hinted, I should insulate myself from what Sergeant Psycho did. When I asked for more detail, they would respond with, "Listen, kid, keep your eyes and ears open. Don't let Lieutenant Doyle involve you in their shit."

"I just came off a hairy mission," I said and was in no mood to translate your hints. "Give it to me straight as to what you are talking about."

"Now that you are in charge of C4, you will get sucked into Lieutenant Doyle's side hustle. If you do, it could be bad news for you."

That night, I was trying to figure out how I could get Psycho's body back and out of Vietnam. I regretted my decision to join the Army. The more I tried to do what was right; I got into deeper shit.

The very least I owed Psycho was to get his body back with proper a military burial. In my mind, I pictured Psycho's lifeless body lying in that clearing surrounded by VC while they argued as to who gets to claim the reward.

While walking around in a drunken haze, my thoughts kept bouncing between retrieving Psycho's body and wondering what kind of stuff Lieutenant Doyle and Psycho were into. Why did the other squad leader give me such a warning? I found myself standing outside the door of the morgue. I wondered what kind of help Lieutenant Doyle could give in getting Psycho's body back.

RECOVERY PLANS

Before that night, I never asked Lieutenant Doyle anything big. She always offered supplies, treats, and advice. I eagerly would escort her and promptly snap pictures when she asked. The little things I did were a small way of paying her back for all she did for us.

It must have been close to midnight when I staggered past the morgue. A light shone from around the door. Only Lieutenant Doyle would be in there this late. I turned the doorknob. It was unlocked. Strange, she usually kept it locked after dark.

I cracked the door open and yelled, "Hello, Lieutenant Doyle. Are you in there?"

"I'm here. Come on in. I've been waiting for you."

Her words surprised me. Little did I know walking through that door would change my life, more than my previous months in Vietnam.

I walked through the hall and stood outside her open office door.

"Don't just stand there. Come on in and have a seat."

Sitting behind her desk, I saw Lieutenant Doyle wipe the

tears from her eyes. Seeing her caused me to fight back tears of my own. Taking a deep sigh, she asked. "Can I help you?"

"What's the matter? What's going on?" I didn't expect her to be so emotional over the loss of Psycho. Only later did I understand the emotional unsaid bond the two had. Psycho and Doyle depended a lot upon each other.

Ignoring my questions "You are in charge of C4, now. Have you come for my help?"

"I would rather have Psycho back and in charge," I said.

Alice Doyle pushed back a flood of tears. "I was expecting you to come by. Since you are in charge now, we have a lot to talk about."

"Yes, we need to talk. I think the first thing we need to discuss is how we can get Psycho's body back?"

"Have a seat over there." Doyle pointed at the folding chair beside her large desk. My drunken haze left me as I sat in that chair.

Suppressing her emotions, she continued. "I know Psycho is dead. I don't blame you for having to leave his body behind. Before we do anything else, I need you to fill me in on what happened."

While I recited the events from the ambush to our extraction, Doyle made me feel comfortable. I felt like we were back in Idaho and sitting at the kitchen table with my mother. My mother and I had this ritual. I would get home from school and tell her about my day. She would sit and listen. Doyle did the same thing. She just sat there in her chair and listened.

When finished, Lieutenant Doyle leaned forward. She reached out to my hand and looked me in the eye. "Sargent Jason Roberts aka Cameraman. I have already started the process of getting Psycho's body back. Tomorrow morning, we will take a little road trip. We will be bringing Psycho's body back."

"When are we going? How...?" Hearing her words filled my

mind with questions. I shouldn't have been surprised. I have often seen her accomplish things I never expected from her.

"It is my job to know a lot of things. From time to time, I have made arrangements on both sides of this war. It is all for the greater good."

At that point in time, it hit me what the squad leaders were trying to tell me. Lieutenant Doyle and Sergeant Psycho did more than cross the line drawn by Army regulations. They dealt with our enemy. I thought that was treason. Means death by firing squad!

"Psycho was a good friend and business associate of mine." I listened, taking in every word she said. "I have lost count of the number of times Psycho helped me. He didn't want personal compensation. He wanted C4 and you to have the benefit of our dealing."

"What do you want from me in exchange for getting Psycho's body back?" I asked, waiting for the big ask.

"This road trip is more like you and me paying back Psycho for all the help he had done."

Right then, like so many other times in Vietnam, I experienced the lines of right and wrong getting blurred for the sake of getting the job done.

Doyle explained. "I have made some arrangements. I need you to meet me at the Motor Pool at zero seven thirty hours tomorrow morning. Bring your camera and two rolls of film. The only weapon you are to be carrying is your sidearm. We are going to take a road trip that will last most of the day, maybe longer.

"You will want to have Sparky take C4 out to the shooting range. That will keep their minds and body busy. Don't tell them what we are going to do."

When Doyle said road trip, I thought back to all the road trips I took with her and Psycho. I like to think on those road trips we became close friends. This road trip will mean something very different.

I left Lieutenant Doyle's office, then turned left and out the back door of the morgue. Walking back to the Hooch left me feeling like I had no choices in my life. Others dictated what I was to do and how I was to do it.

ROAD TRIP

The next morning, I arranged for Sparky to take C4 to the firing range. I figured if they were busy at the firing range, they would be less likely to get into trouble. Captain Phillips wouldn't be looking for me or finding a reason to send us out on another mission. I would not put it past the Captain to send us out shorthanded and with no downtime to morn Psycho.

1968 saw the death of 16,899 American soldiers. The highest number of all the years we were in South Vietnam. Soldiers stationed at Da Nang, like us, purposely ignored the weekly death totals. We didn't want to think about death. We wanted to get back home.

At zero-seven thirty hours, I arrived at the motor pool. Lieutenant Alice Doyle was already sitting on the passenger's side of a Willys Jeep, with it running. She looked at me as if I was late. She had the duty clerk strap two extra gas tanks on the back of the Jeep.

Dressed in faded olive greens, Lieutenant Doyle had her hair stuffed into an olive green cap. At first glance, anyone would have trouble telling if she was a man or a woman. They had to examine her throat for an Adam's Apple.

When she saw me, she motioned for me to get directly into the driver's seat. "You're late. I already checked the Jeep out for the day. Let's go."

The Army had trained me to thoroughly check out whatever I was driving. Kicking the tires along with checking the oil and water went unsaid. Out of respect for the lieutenant, I only tapped the extra cans. They were full. Then I unscrewed the lids. I stuck my nose close to the opening to verify they held gas, not water or diesel.

"Yes, they are full of gasoline. I even check the engine oil and water myself." I could tell Lieutenant Doyle got perturbed with me. "Now, get in. We have a full day's journey ahead of us."

"Why so much gas?" I asked.

"We are going to need it for the return trip."

I set my camera bag behind the driver's seat. I also noticed a rut sack and a field walkie-talkie back there.

"Where are we headed?" I asked.

"Drive west toward Thuong Duc. You will turn before we get to the Ashuau Valley. After that, I will have to guide you to the exact location."

"Shouldn't we have more weapons other than my sidearm? There are NVA patrols throughout that area."

"I have made arrangements. I have struck up a deal with my counterpart in that area. They have guaranteed us safe passage for the sole purpose of retrieving Psycho's body."

I had learned never to question Lieutenant Doyle. No matter how much I wanted to understand what she did and why. I had to trust her and pray we would not get killed or captured.

Where we got ambushed resulting in leaving Psycho's body was much further south than where Lieutenant Doyle directed me to drive. I kept my eyes on the road and listened for her directions.

We passed through Thuong Duc. The villagers gave us some

strange looks as we drove through. A mile or so later, we came across a patrol of South Vietnamese Army soldiers and two American advisers. They moved to the side of the road so we could pass.

Doyle pointed forty feet ahead of us. "Turn right on that dirt road up there."

"Yes, ma'am."

I made the turn. The road got a little rougher. I had to let off the gas.

A couple of hours later, she asked, "Are you getting hungry?"

"A little. I'm more focused on getting Psycho's body and getting back to base." Being in the middle of enemy territory with only a semi-automatic sidearm didn't help my appetite.

Lieutenant Doyle reached around behind us and pulled out the rut sack. "I brought us something to eat while we are on the road." She opened the sack revealing two sandwiches and a couple cans of Royal Crown Cola.

"I bought a couple of peanut butter and jelly sandwiches with your favorite soda. The peanut butter has been spread on the bottom slice of bread and strawberry jelly on top, just the way you like it." She flashed me a smile. I always wondered if she felt the same way about me as I did about her. That smile confirmed my suspicions.

"Thank you," I said, returning her smile.

I ate my sandwich between turns and bumps in the road. After every couple of bites, she took my sandwich and handed me the soda. I took a sip and handed it back to her. She would hand me back my partially eaten sandwich.

After those sandwiches were eaten, we made small talk for the next several miles. The road got narrower as it snaked around the side of the mountains. The left side of the road dropped off to a hundred feet or more.

MORE SCHOOLING

"Don't think what I do is easy." Lieutenant Doyle confessed. "Last night, before you showed up at my door, I had been working on getting Psycho's body back. I had made contact with my North Vietnamese counterpart. He got in contact with the commander, who has Psycho's body. Then we agreed on the place for us to meet and the conditions of the exchange were tough."

"Do I really need to know what you are telling me?" I asked.

"It will help you understand what will transpire today."

"What is going to happen? I thought we were just picking up Psycho's body."

"I will not answer all the questions you have about how I made this arrangement. What I want you to know is we have one thing working in our favor."

"What's that?"

"The bounty on Psycho's head. Hanoi wants it on display at the capitol building. That made it easier for me to make the right discreet inquiries. We are going to make a simple trade for Psycho's body."

"What are we trading?"

"It is better said a kind of trade?" Hearing those words made me go from cautious to worried. I couldn't imagine what we could be trading, that they would want.

"Psycho trusted you. He said you were a good guy. We both know you had a bad break with General Moorehead. Psycho went out of his way to teach you the basics. He believed you would make an excellent sergeant and squad leader. Today, you are going to see more of what it is like to fill his shoes."

"What are you talking about?" My mind kept wanting to find out what kind of trade Doyle meant. "What is this about a trade?" I almost stopped the jeep. I feared I had gotten involved with something I didn't want any part of.

Everything from boot camp to sending the General's wife the picture of the General and his mistress kissing could not equal the shit Lieutenant Doyle implied while I drove that jeep.

"Jason, Sergeant Roberts, I have arranged for you to take pictures of Psycho's body and to exchange the film and camera for Psycho's body."

I didn't know what to say. I just kept driving. Finally, I asked. "Who did you make this arrangement with?" I took a breath. "Who are we meeting to do this trade?"

"The North Vietnamese officer in charge of transporting Psycho's body to Hanoi."

"Oh, shit," I blurted out of my mouth. "Why would he want to make such a trade with us?"

"Well, Jason, in this heat and humidity, a dead body will smell rather quickly. Psycho has already been dead for a couple of days. I assure you he must be smelling pretty ripe by now."

"The North Vietnamese Army officer would rather take your camera and pictures than take Psycho's smelly dead the rest of the way to Hanoi for the bounty."

I didn't argue with Lieutenant Doyle about giving up my camera for Psycho's body. I could always requisition another camera. At least we could see Psycho getting buried with full military honors. The thought of putting Psycho in for a fancy metal flag-draped casket lingered in my mind.

The harder I tried to make sense of my life in Vietnam, the more it didn't. All I knew was the one man who taught me how to survive in Nam was dead. I was driving a Jeep with a half Japanese and half white Army nurse with the rank of lieutenant. She sometimes acts more like my girlfriend than my superior officer. From time to time, she would tell me how to get around military rules and regulations. Other times, she would emphasize the need for rules and why we should follow them.

From the first time I met her and every time I would get around her, my face would feel flush and my blood would boil. She forced me to change my perception of life and reality. Still, I had a feeling she was keeping a lot of information from me. The safe thing for me to do would be for me not to ask too many questions.

During that road trip, she told me things I only suspected were true. "My CIA contact in Laos in turn contacted their counterpart with the North Vietnamese Army in Cambodia. That operative contacted the North Vietnamese Army officer, who had the task of transporting Psycho's body up to Hanoi to collect the bounty."

Lieutenant Alice Doyle continued to give me all the details of what she had arranged. "Fortunately, the North Vietnamese Army officer didn't like the idea of transporting a smelly dead body all the way to Hanoi. He made it known he wanted a nice camera to take pictures of his adventures. When I suggested to him that pictures of the body and camera in exchange for Psycho's body, he agreed."

RECOVERY

After five and a half hours, we arrived at our destination. Lieutenant Doyle had me park the jeep on the edge of a burned-out village. The sight and smell of the burned-out made our job more unpleasant. I did see a couple of places where green vegetation sprouted from the ashes. From the other signs, I guessed the village got napalmed about a year ago. The awful sickening smell of napalm still lingered.

I have walked through hillsides and the jungle in ash from napalm. This was the first time for me to see an entire village destroyed from napalm. Seeing and smelling it never gets easy.

I will never forget the sight of burned bodies and animals. The burned corpses were just left to rot. No one came back to bury them. The scorched ground will always remind me of the horror that happened to that village.

Lieutenant Doyle instructed me, "I want you to get your camera out. Take some pictures of what you see here. Save that rollback for when they arrive. Put a second roll of film for when we make the trade."

I didn't tell Doyle. I had brought four rolls of film instead of two as she had requested. In the back of my mind, I wanted to keep some of these pictures for myself. I thought it might be beneficial to have a photo record of our road trip and this burned-out village.

It didn't take long for us to hear the feet heading in our direction. The Lieutenant and myself turned our heads toward the far end of the village's remains. I lowered my right hand to unsnap the cover over my sidearm. Doyle rested her hand over mine, preventing me from pulling my weapon out.

From the jungle emerged nine men. They all wore the uniform of the North Vietnamese Army. In the lead, the man had two gold bars on his collar. In his hand, an AK-47 pointed in the air like the other men. Only the two carrying a stretcher had their rifles hanging off their shoulders.

Before we got to the village, Lieutenant Doyle reminded me that American soldiers travel with their rifle muzzle pointing down. North Vietnamese travel with their rifle muzzle pointing up. That is why so many American soldiers had trouble with dirt getting in and plugging their rifle barrels.

The two North Vietnamese soldiers carried a bamboo stretcher. On the stretcher rested a dirty black body bag. From the bulge of the body bag, we could only conclude it held Psycho's body.

My camera hung around my neck. I kept my right hand resting on the top of my sidearm. Ready to pull it out at any moment. If they were going to kill Doyle or me, I was going to take out as many as I could before they had a chance.

The two men carrying the stretcher set it on the ground between their group and us. One carrier bent over and unzipped the body bag. It took everything within me to contain myself while snapping photos of Psycho's lifeless body.

Doyle put her hand on my upper arm. "Put a fresh roll of film in your camera. Take some more pictures of Psycho and these soldiers. Then give them the camera and the film that is in the camera."

I did almost as Doyle asked. When finished, I handed the NVA captain the camera. He motioned for his men to place Psycho's body and the stretcher on the back of the jeep. As quickly as the nine appeared, they disappeared into the jungle.

ON THE WAY BACK

I emptied both gas cans into the Jeep's gas tank. Doyle made sure the stretcher and Psycho's body would ride securely back to Da Nang.

Before we left, Lieutenant Doyle asked, "Do you remember how to get back?"

I nodded. During most of the trip back, neither one of us said a word. Except she would remind me which turn I should take.

I made a brief nod. Neither one of us felt like making even a casual conversation.

We got ten minutes outside the village we had passed through earlier. Lieutenant Doyle broke the silence again. "You need to go a little faster. You are driving like we are in a funeral procession."

I glanced at her as to say, "Aren't we?"

She must have realized what she said, and it didn't come out right. "I mean, you need to drive a little faster. We have to get back to the base before dark."

At one point, I began to turn on a paved road. She corrected me. "Don't turn here. You will need to take the right in another hundred yards."

"How do you know? Where is the map you are looking at?"

"I got a photographic memory. All I need to do is look at a map and have it memorized."

"Do you have all of Vietnam memorized?" I asked.

"Just the area where we are traveling today."

We approach an American Army patrol resting on the side of the road. As we approached, they all stood up and came to attention. As we passed, they saluted. I always wondered if they knew we were carrying Psycho's body in the back of our jeep.

The west gate of Da Nang came into sight, and then just out of nowhere, we got hit with a downpour of rain. That was an uncommon occurrence for that time of the year.

The guard at the gate smiled at us. "You two look like a couple of wet rats." Then he waved us through. He saluted as we passed.

I pulled up to the morgue entrance, just as the sun had set below the jungle. Lieutenant Doyle volunteered a couple of passing soldiers to take the Psycho's body inside. She followed them in. I went to the Motor Pool to drop off the Jeep.

Afterward, I went back to the morgue. Then I walked Alice Doyle to her barracks. Outside her barracks, she asked. "Can I get the roll of film that you took from the burned-out village?"

"Yes, I was going to develop it in the morning and then take the prints to you."

"What about that second roll of film? I saw you swapped out before handing the camera to the North Vietnamese captain?"

"Uh, so you saw me make the switch?"

"Mister Roberts, you are not as slick as you think you are. You are lucky the captain didn't catch you making the switch."

"It will be a couple of days before he can get the film developed."

"Tell me, what was on that roll of film you put in the camera?"

"Nothing, it was an empty roll. I figured he could take some pictures on his way up to Hanoi."

"You sneaky bastard," Alice gave me a big smile. "I like it. Don't forget to bring me those prints when you get them developed tomorrow."

I gave her a salute. "Yes, ma'am."

The next day, C4 spent the morning cleaning and doing busy work around the Hooch. I headed over to my darkroom. I wanted to develop both rolls of film and print copies for Doyle and myself before noon.

I made it back to the Hooch shortly after zero eleven hundred hours. Everyone but Shadow was sitting around drinking beer. After Ruben and Mick got transferred to the Da Nang hospital. They released Ruben. Mick checked himself out and limped his way back. They were all on their way to getting a good buzz.

MOURNING OUR LOSS

I never expected to inherit the duties of a parent at twenty-one. That's how I felt watching C4 sit around getting buzzed in the middle of the afternoon. Not one teenager among them, but six men acted and talked like teenagers drinking beer and getting rowdy. Inside, I wished I could be one of them. No, I wanted to be back in Idaho shoveling horse shit out of my uncle's barn.

"We got word Shadow's wounds were serious," Mick said. "They are shipping him to the hospital in Hawaii. Chances are they will send him home with a Purple Heart and an Honorable Discharge."

Ruben had a flesh wound that tore some skin. The doctors gave him a couple of stitches and sent him back to us. I put in the paperwork for him to get a purple heart.

Mick is a hardass in more ways than one. When he dropped his pants, the bullet fell on the floor. The doctor said he didn't need any stitches. They wanted to keep Mick for a couple of days, but he left. He said some of the nurses teased him about having a hard ass. I always wanted to hear Mick explain to his family back home how he got his purple heart.

The next morning, I took C4 out to the firing range. When I saw everyone was shooting better than usual, I smiled. I knew we would get orders at any time to head out into the jungle.

A Staff Sergeant, from Central Command North showed up late that afternoon. We were kicking back, resting from spending most of the day on the firing range. He announced to the squad and me. "I need you deadbeats stand up, get presentable, and follow me."

"Why? What's up?" I asked.

"Just follow me," He barked. I rarely heard that sergeant bark orders with such coldness.

We followed him across the base in a signal file. We must have looked like a bunch of baby ducks following the mother duck.

We marched into the NCO club. Once inside the door, our eyes landed on a metal casket with soldiers from every branch of the military gathered around. I notice a few from the South Vietnamese unit station at Da Nang, too. They directed us to stand along the wall at the head of the casket.

Colonel Beck stepped to the head of the casket. For an officer, that morning he had trouble finding words. "We, we, gather here to pay our respects to a fallen brother in arms. He --- he, didn't always do everything according to regulations or follow orders. I found out early I could count on him to get done whatever needed to be done."

"When did he ever do anything according to regulations?" I heard Mick blurted out.

The Colonel ignored the comment and continued. "I am sure everyone here respected Sergeant Psycho. Does anyone remember hearing his real name? I don't. I saw it twice, but I don't remember it."

The Colonel took a deep breath. "I know it is hard to trust someone who goes by the handle of Psycho when his squad's radio call sign is Psych Ward. I know he is up to some pretty crazy shit. However, whatever needed to be done, he made sure it got done.

Certain individuals in command wished for Psycho's death. God knows, The North Vietnamese and Viet Cong definitely did. The bounty on his head was the highest of any American soldier to date.

I believe all of us wished he had not walked out into that field. Because Psycho has so affected our lives, we had to arrange this memorial here."

Colonel Beck stepped back. Lieutenant Doyle stepped to the head of the casket. "Sergeant Psycho worked hard to make sure his squad would come ba-ba-back——." Doyle's voice cracked. Her eyes filled with tears. Bowing her head, she stepped back. I could see her struggling to fight back a tidal wave of emotion.

Beck invited me to step forward and say a few words. I don't remember the words I said. All I knew was they were inadequate. After my lame attempt, he invited each member of C4 to say something. That was the most emotion I had ever seen out of those guys.

Soldiers see the results of war every day in a buddy getting shot, or a limb blown off, or the icy stare from a lifeless body. We stood there in solemn silence for the one man who in this hell hole affected so many lives in a positive way. That memorial service was put together by soldiers who wanted one. Central Command remained unaware of our actions until its completion.

We all knew the brass would block any recommendation for Psycho to get the Congressional Medal of Honor. The idea made me sick. The only recognition he would get was that metal casket and the American flag draped over it.

INTERESTING INTEL

After all the words of the memorial were said, most everyone headed back to their duty station. A few remained. I stood with my back against a wall, observing how other soldiers suppressed their grief. In the opposite corner of the room, Lieutenant Doyle motioned for me to go to her.

"Is there anything I can do for you?" I asked.

She reached around my waist and gave me a big hug. She held that position to the point I felt uncomfortable. Then she stepped back and stiffened herself. "This morning, I got some interesting intel." The lieutenant put on her face of a superior officer. "I think you might be interested in hearing."

"What is that?"

"Your favorite general has not learned his lesson. He now has a mistress in Saigon, along with running a protection racket on local shopkeepers."

"That is not surprising." I knew she wanted to get the news off her chest, but all I could think about was Psycho and how much I already missed him.

"But there is more."

"What more than that could there be?"

"Your beloved Captain Phillips does not visit whore houses. When in Saigon he visits those of his sex."

Hearing the words Doyle said, I went from grief grief-filled haze to renewed anger for my commanding officer. "What does that do with me? They are down in Saigon, and I am up here in Da Nang. I can't do anything thing about their shit."

"Just keep it filed away for future reference. In the meantime. I have a present for you."

She took the large bag hanging off her shoulder and handed it to me. "Here this is to replace the camera you traded for Sergeant Psycho's body."

I took the bag and looked inside. I had given the same model of camera to the North Vietnamese officer. Knowing how long it would take to get it, meant she had to of ordered it before we left on our road trip.

I had to smile. "Thank you." Seeing my reaction, she smiled, and then my smile got bigger.

"Why are you smiling so big?" She asked.

"You got me a replacement camera, and I flashed on that NVA officer's face when he found out there was nothing on the roll of film I left in the camera."

A smile came over Doyle's face. "Now you have a camera. It may be an ideal time to take a road trip down to Saigon."

"If you are implying what I think you are implying, I have learned my lesson. You can count me out. I am not pointing this camera in General Moorehead's direction."

"Come on, it would be fun. I know some people in Washington who would love to see some of your recent work with General Moorehead as the principal subject."

"Fun! I am afraid of what else the General will do to me."

"Where you messed up in Germany was by sending the photograph to the wrong location. If you take the pictures, let me send them off. I will guarantee you they will have maximum effect."

"Does that mean we are both getting shot for treason?"

"No, that does not mean we are going to get shot. You got to trust me." When Lieutenant Doyle said trust me, I got so nervous, I had to leave her at the NCO club.

Later that evening, back at C4's hooch, someone delivered a bottle of Jack Daniels. The entire squad finished the bottle by drinking shots back-to-back.

A couple of the guys got concerned, for they had to invite me when it came time to take another shot of that whiskey. I wasn't morning over Psycho. In reality, I was trying to forget what Lieutenant Doyle told me. I knew what she had in mind for us taking a road trip to Saigon. Inside, I liked the idea, but all I could think about was her plan going wrong. I had a more important responsibility to the squad. Inwardly, I was getting pulled in two directions. The knot in my stomach would not go away.

IN CHARGE

The next morning, dread filled the air. A dark storm cloud moved over the western portion of the base. All morning, no one spoke more than a word or two at the most. None of us felt like going to the mess hall. Dave had coffee brewing out back.

I knew my first job would be to get the men's minds off of Psycho's death. Not one man in the squad was happy about the ambush and how Central Command delayed our EVAC.

Right after zero nine hundred hours, the front door of our hooch flew open. From outside came a loud, "Attention!" Instinctively, we all looked in that direction. and scrabbled to stand in front of our bunks. In walked Captain Phillips, flanked by his favorite blond-haired sergeant.

Captain Phillips walked past each of us. Only stopping long enough to give each one of us a contemptuous eye. We stayed at attention only out of respect for the uniform and rank. Certainly not for the man.

Finally, Captain Phillips positioned himself directly in front of me. "I am curious. Did Sergeant Psycho take the bullet meant for you?"

I didn't answer.

"Well, Roberts, I see you have survived thus far. That means you get another field promotion. You are now Squad Leader to this group of misfits."

I changed my posture from the traditional stiff attention to an at-ease stance. "But sir, I am not qualified. There are other members in this squad with a lot more experience than me. Anyone of them could do a much better job than me."

"Psycho trained you to take his place. If he didn't, I wouldn't be talking to you."

Captain Phillips put his nose one inch from mine. For a moment in time, I thought he was going to kiss me. Putting his right foot behind his left, he spun himself around and took two steps. Then he again put his right foot behind his left and spun himself around again.

"Listen, Mister Roberts, you don't question my orders. Every man in this squad has held the rank of sergeant. They all got busted to private because they couldn't handle the job. I want to see if you can do any better than what they have done."

The Captain took a step closer. He leaned forward and whispered in my ear. "As far as General Moorehead and I are concerned, this whole squad should be laying on the hilltop somewhere, peppered with holes, while having the local collection of bugs and animals feasting off your flesh."

Looking down the line at the members of C4, he raised his voice. "Maybe someone from this squad can shoot you. That way, they can put you out of your misery. It will make the General and myself happy. I am sure General Moorehead will gladly give that soldier a promotion and reassignment stateside."

After a moment of silence, Captain Phillips did a snappy ninety-degree turn, nodded to his sergeant, and walked out.

"Sir! Sir!" came the words out of my mouth.

The Captain stopped. His back to me. "What is it, Sergeant?"

"Can we get a week of stand-down time to grieve and regroup?"

"No, you have already had enough downtime. I have a mission for the fourth squad. You will board two Hueys tomorrow at nineteen hundred hours. Fourth Squad will do recon and mapping branches on the Ho Chi Minh Trail. We have gotten reports of large groups of troops and supplies coming down from the north. Expect to be in the field for at least a week." Captain Phillips continued out. His sergeant slammed the door shut so hard that it bounced.

Everyone in the squad exchanged glances and then at me. I tried pushing back the paranoid thoughts. No matter how hard I tried, my mind flooded with picturing who would take the Captain up on his offer and kill me.

I asked myself who would off me and when. Would it be Ruben, the tough gang member from LA? Would it be Mick, the New York hardass? Before I showed up, he was Psycho's second. It could be Sparky. He is always looking to blow something up. Why not me? I didn't have to worry about Dave. All he wanted to do was smoke dope and keep everyone happy. I don't think Leroy would do it. He liked to have someone else in charge. I could not see Pham, our Vietnamese translator, wanting the responsibility. He would only do it if the rest of the squad agreed to it.

"You can relax, Sarge." came the words out of Sparky's mouth. "We are not going to kill you."

Mick added. "The Captain gave us the same speech the day Psycho took charge. We will obey your orders if nothing else to spite the Captain."

Regardless of Mick's words, I felt the weight of being responsible for the squad. I wished Psycho was alive and I could lean on his experience.

DOYLE REALLY DOES

"Sarge, this ammo is crap. The 5.56mm ammo they issued us for these M16's keeps jamming. We can only get off four rounds before it jams." Mick yelled at me.

"Can we get back some ammo for our CAR-15's?" added Ruben.

Sparky walked up to me. He held out pieces of a claymore mine. "This claymore looks like a leftover from World War I. I'm afraid it will go off just from the vibration of a Huey ride."

Hearing everyone complain about our downgraded equipment made me wish someone would shoot me. Let someone else deal with all the frustration. Mick likened out M16s to being worse than BB guns. The way he talked made me think BB guns would have made the squad happier. Damm if I was going to take C4 on a mission with BB guns.

In the early evening, I went to see Lieutenant Doyle. I needed to vent. I knew she would be the only one I could openly vent. Getting deployed with the junk they gave us meant by nightfall we would be dead.

I walked into the morgue as Doyle closed the lid on a casket.

For a minute, she stood there staring at it. She showed concern when she asked. "What's up, Jason?"

"I'm frustrated." I blurred it out.

"What's happening?"

"Our ammo is garbage. Sparky says the claymores and other explosives are too unstable to ride in a chopper. I need to know how we can get back the ammo and explosives you were supplying us."

She took a deep breath. "It will not be easy. You may not like how Psycho and I were getting them."

"Right now, I don't care. I'm responsible for keeping those guys alive. I need and will take every advantage you can give me."

Doyle motioned me to follow her back to her office.

"Close the door and have a seat. I have something important I need to tell you." The way she said it, I knew I would not like the next words out of her mouth.

Lieutenant Doyle sat on the edge of her desk. "You know, I will you do anything to get the same weapons and ammo that those Special Forces operators use. It will be best that you or anyone in the squad don't ask how I do it."

"If it means keeping each member of the squad alive. Do it!"

"What I need to tell you is not common knowledge." When she said those words, I felt like she needed to confess to me a big secret. "Only a select few on this base know what I am going to tell you. I'm depending upon you to keep it that way."

I raised and lowered my head as to say yes. I stiffened my body and took a deep breath. Now I was ready to handle whatever shocking revelation came my way.

"Remember when you flew to Da Nang with Psycho and me?"

"Yes, in the C130."

"Remember the boxes with my name on them?"

"Yes, I remember they were body bags?"

"The body bags were covering ammo for C4. Other times, there were claymores and rifles."

"Oh," was all I could say. I suspected, but never heard it said out loud.

"We had a connection with the supply depot stateside. We got from them certain things underneath body bags."

"Can you re-establish that connection?"

"If I can re-establish that arrangement, but it will be a week or more before we get anything. I think it is time you know exactly how we got all the specialty weapons and ammo for C4."

At that point, I wished she would just spell it out. I could hear the reluctance in her voice.

"I put heroin in caskets with the dead soldiers. At the other end, they take the heroin out and sell it on the street. That money is used to pay for specialty weapons and ammo sent to me under body bags. I give it to you and C4."

My mouth fell open. I could not believe the words Lieutenant Alice Doyle said. She smuggled drugs into the states to pay for our guns and ammo.

I nervously asked, "How did you obtain the heroin?" After those words were out of my mouth, I wish I had kept my mouth shut.

"Psycho would pick it up for me on one of his off-base errands."

"Why did you and him stop?"

"Psycho wanted to shield you. He figured being his second, you would eventually find out."

"Is there anything you can do to help us before tomorrow?" At that point, I didn't care. I just wanted to get everyone back from our next mission alive.

Her expression changed several times. I could tell she ran

every option she could think of. "I might get you something before you leave out."

"Anything is better than what we got now."

"There is one idea."

"What is that?" I asked.

"North Vietnamese Army usually has pretty good weapons and ammo. After your first firefight, take their weapons and ammo, then use it."

"The problem with that is winning that first firefight. What we have now only ensures us losing."

"Let me see what I can do. I can't really promise anything until you guys get back. In the meantime, I am going to work on getting some ammo delivered to your hooch before you leave."

I walked out of Lieutenant Alice Doyle's office in a daze. The one woman I admired and fantasized over supplies heron to junkies back in the states. Granted, she used the money from the heroin sales to buy C4 high quality weapons, ammo, and explosives. It seemed so wrong for us to contribute to a junky strung out on the sidewalks in New York City just to support us killing communist in Southeast Asia.

LAST MINUTE PREP

The next morning, I woke up to banging at the back entrance to our hooch. It was still dark outside. I opened the door to see the big grizzly soldier from Dog Patch, who liked to pick on me. On the ground behind him were three wooden crates.

"I got a special delivery here for you from Santa Claus. Come out here and get them. I don't want anyone seeing me doing this delivery."

Dave and Leroy ran past me and grabbed one crate each. I watched them pass me and set the crates on the table in the supply room. I grabbed the third crate and said, "Thank you." Before taking my crate inside.

By that time, the rest of the squad had gathered in the supply room. Dave and Leroy already had opened their crates. I wasn't far behind them. Christmas had come early for us.

Anyone watching us would have thought we were a bunch of kids on Christmas morning. Sparky pulled out claymores fresh from the factory. Dave pulled out several banana clips of ammo. Leroy found the special ammo he liked for his sniper rifle. Mick took over, going through Dave's crate. A cloud of disappointment hung over Dave.

"What's a matter?" I asked Dave.

"We got all this stuff to kill and maim, but no medical supplies."

"Hey Sarge, you really came through for us," Leroy yelled out, ignoring Dave's concerns. "This is the top-notch ammo. This is the kind only the black op operators get." Leroy held up two more ammo clips.

"Fill your packs and store the rest," I said. "We need to go to breakfast and act like we didn't get these supplies. I want as few people as possible to know about this delivery."

"Sarge, did these come from Lieutenant Doyle?" Dave asked. "Do you think she can get us some medical supplies? We're running low."

I didn't know what to say. I just smiled. Then I thought it best to say something. "After breakfast, you and I will go by the base hospital and see what we can get."

Mick added. "We don't want to know what you and Lieutenant Doyle had to do to get this stuff. My gut tells me it wasn't good."

Leroy injected, "I personally don't like the Lieutenant. Anyone who hangs around all those dead bodies. That creeps me out."

Mick looked directly at me and said, "I think I can speak for the entire squad. If anyone can help us when we are in the jungle, it is much appreciated."

Sparky waved bars of plastic explosive in the air. "I don't mean to change the subject. We have to stop talking and get some work done. Sarge is right, we need to get this stuff stored away and get some breakfast. We are looking at a long day."

We consumed what the cooks called breakfast. It was composed of sausage and powdered scrambled eggs. Certainly not home cooking, but better than canned C-rations. At least in the field they issued us those new MRE. Lighter and all we had to do was add water.

Back at the Hooch, we prepared for our next mission. The same thing we did hundreds of times before. Everyone still checked and double checked what they carried. I had each member verify what another squad member carried. I didn't want any surprises.

Sparky wanted to test one of his Christmas presents. Leroy wanted to fire off a couple of rounds, along with everyone else. I sent them to the firing range while I checked in at Central Command.

While at Central Command North. I wanted to confirm the Landing Zone and extraction point. In my mind, knowing those two exact points would eliminate any surprises. I double checked our call signs and travel route. Getting caught in the middle of any napalm run would be disastrous.

The staff sergeant wanted to change our squad's call sign to Dead Beats. I convinced him we should keep it as "Psych Ward", out of respect for Psycho. My personal call sign stayed the same.

"Is there anything else I need to know about our mission?" I asked.

"You got everything I know about."

"I don't want to have a delay on EVAC like last time."

"Your little hike looks like it won't be too eventful."

As I reached to door, the sergeant shouted at me, "As long as you don't do any of that crazy shit like Psycho. Everything should go smoothly."

I turned and gave him a stare. "I will try not to."

We were late getting to the two Hueys waiting for us. This was our first time going out without Psycho. All of us were nervous. I prayed everyone wasn't as nervous as me.

THE AMBUSH

I jumped out of the first Huey and ran ten feet before kneeling. Mick took up a position on my right with the radio. In that moment of realization, I felt a panic rise within me. I had my camera back at the Hooch. The whole time with C4, I had a camera around my neck or in my backpack. I was so attentive to have the squad ready for deployment; I left behind the one thing I carried with me on every mission.

By nature, I am not a superstitious person. Considering what transpired on that mission, I wish I had taken the extra time to get my camera.

The sun had reached a midpoint in the sky on the second day. We came upon what looked like a rather large campsite situated twenty-five feet off to one side of the trail. We didn't see any NVA or Viet Cong. It looked as if they used it for an overnight stopover.

We took up a position so no one could see us from the trail or campsite. I placed myself where I could see most of the campsite and the trail coming from Laos. I directed the squad to arrange the branches and leaves so we could have a good place to hang out for the rest of the day and night. If we got lucky, we could ambush a caravan coming in from Laos.

As sunset approached, I felt a tap on my shoulder. Leroy pointed west along the trail. Thirty or more North Vietnamese Army regulars in signal file trekking in our direction. They were all wearing new clean uniforms. In addition to them wearing clean uniforms, they stepped with a snappiness that told me they were fresh, well-trained replacements. I knew, right away, our work was cut out for us.

The two in front looked more experienced by the way they examined the trail for booby traps. Following them was a column pushing bicycles. Tied to the bicycles were bundles and crates. Ten soldiers followed them, carrying AK-47s.

We shot each other a smile. We had hit the jackpot. As the caravan settled in at the campsite, I gave members of C4 hand signals to position themselves. If we were to take out this whole caravan, we would have to be smart. I was hoping they would be too tired from the day's march to notice C4 getting into position.

As soon as the caravan reached the campsite, they went right to work, fixing their evening meal of rice. We waited and watched them for the next two hours. I wanted to wait until they were comfortable with their guard down. Just before dark, the vast majority of them already had a full stomach and were ready to go asleep. I knew our surprise attack would be the most effective after they were asleep.

As squad leader, I had the responsibility to make the decision as to what we were to do and when we were to do it. If we moved into an attack position too soon, and get discovered before we were ready, would mean disaster.

I motioned for Ruben and Sparky to move to a better position. Mick passed the radio to Dave, then got into position. I signaled Dave to make sure he turned the radio off and bend the antenna down. I didn't want any unnecessary noise giving our position away. Then I motioned for Pham to my right side because I wanted him to listen and let me know what they were saying.

I knew Sparky, Ruben, and Mick were a little crazy. They wouldn't hold back when the firefight got going. I had Ruben to my far left and Mick to do the same to my far right. Sparky positioned himself so he could drop grenades into the center of their camp. I didn't want any of them to escape when the bullets started flying.

Sparky got himself in a position where he could place his grenades where they would do the most good. He set in a row six grenades next to him. Then Sparky looked at me and raised a grenade, signaling he was ready. He knew his primary target would be in the center of their camp. After that, he would be tossing grenades toward the line of bicycles and their packages.

Leroy moved back a safe distance, but close enough to take out anyone trying to escape. He found the perfect spot behind a fallen tree to rest his sniper rifle.

Without warning, I heard a loud snap from behind me. Dave shot me a look, like the cat who ate the canary. He took the radio off his back and set down on a branch that snapped.

A NVA guard stood up and looked in our direction. He lowered his weapon in Dave's direction. I don't think he saw Dave, because he took a few steps looking for the source of the sound, then went back to where he was sitting.

I saw another North Vietnamese soldier walk in my direction. He stopped six feet from my head. I lifted my CAR-15 and aimed it directly at his groin. He looked past me like I wasn't there, but when he looked down, I pulled the trigger. He fell back. His AK let off several rounds.

POST AMBUSH

Sparky took me shooting the nosey soldier as the signal for him to start tossing grenades. Alerted, those relaxing rose to their feet. They looked stunned. I heard a pop from Leroy's rifle. He took out one guard. The rest of C4 went to work doing what they were trained to do. Those NVA soldiers looked more like a bunch of cockroaches scrambling for cover than soldiers.

Sparky landed several well-placed grenades among the bicycles. Mick and Ruben didn't give any of the NVAs time to get their weapons before taking them out. Pham and I did our share of dropping those running for cover. Dave selected the remaining soldiers, who ran up the trail from where they came.

Minutes later, I signaled for the gunfire to stop. I didn't see any movement among the campers. The smell of gunpowder and blood filled the humid air.

Each member of C4 rose to their feet while waiting for some movement. A smile came over all our faces. C4 had taken out over thirty NVA without getting one member of our squad wounded or killed. We had just executed a textbook ambush.

I had come a long way from taking photographs over the Berlin wall to leading a group of misfits. The Army gave me the

MOS of 25 Victory. Otherwise known as Combat Documentation/Production Specialist. I had grown and changed to something far beyond my wildest dreams. Now I am an 11 Baker squad leader.

Our only obvious wounded was Dave's pride for dropping the radio on some dry branches. That snapping sound set the perfect ambush in motion. A little earlier than what I wanted, but we won.

"Sir, look over there," said Pham, pointing to two kneeling with hands on their heads. "We have prisoners."

"You and Mick tie their hands behind their back. Check for weapons. I don't want them giving us any surprises."

Then I directed the rest of the squad to make sure none of the dead were playing dead, waiting to surprise us when we're not looking.

My next order was for Dave to double check everyone in the squad for injuries. I have seen soldiers not realize they were wounded until hours or days later. The adrenaline rush from a firefight can mask some serious pain from wounds.

Ruben felt something wet on his side. He put his hand against his right side. When he pulled it away, he saw blood on his hand. He shouted, "Dave, I need your help over here now!"

Dave ran over to Ruben. He took Dave's med kit. Lifting Ruben's shirt, Dave saw blood seeping out from the middle of his rib cage. Closer examination revealed two holes in Ruben's side.

Dave chuckled when he said. "You sure do like to attract stray bullets. You're lucky the bullet went in and out, striking no serious organs. It looks like it only went skin deep."

Ruben asked. "All I want to know is, am I going to get another Purple Heart and some R and R?"

"You probably will along with some down time in Da Nang. I don't think you are going to get any R and R time, like in

Hawaii." Dave continued wrapping Ruben's midsection with a field dressing.

It took a while before I could get a radio relay back to Central Command North. I had to wait for one of those flies over planes to relay my radio transmission.

From time to time, we would get out of radio range. The US military would have little signal engine planes flying over the areas where we were patrolling. Their job was to assist with recon from the air. Depending upon the patrol's location, the plane would relay radio transmissions.

I smiled when I heard over the radio, "Cameraman, what is your status?"

"Psych Ward just ruined the lives of a convoy full of crazies. We have two prisoners and one wounded."

"How bad is your wounded?"

"He will need at least a few stitches and a Purple Heart."

"What is your position?"

I replied with our coordinates. He came back with an EVAC location that was five clicks away. I checked my map. I wanted to see what kind of terrain between us and the EVAC point. From what I could tell, it would be well after dark before we could get there.

"Is there any place closer?" I radioed.

"That is the closest place where we can get a chopper to you. There are no other clearings unless you want us to do a burn."

I didn't have to think for long. What suggested on the other end meant a jet dropping napalm to clear an area for EVAC. I dismissed the idea. If the pilot drop site was a little off, it would mean C4 would be burnt toast.

GET MOVING

We hadn't reached the halfway to our EVAC point when it got too dark to travel. I wanted to get as much distance as possible between us and the ambush site. I feared an NVA patrol would check on the caravan, then come after us for payback.

After we set up camp, I briefed the guys on how I wanted the EVAC to go. Mick, Dave, Ruben, and one of our two prisoners would take the first chopper. Leroy, Pham, Sparky, me and the other prisoner would go in the second one.

Just after sunrise, the next morning when we were able to get within sight of our EVAC point. I sent Mick and Pham to check out the area.

We had our prisoners' hands tied behind their backs. We looped one end of a rope around their necks and the other end around his buddy's neck. Two feet of rope separated them. Another rope wrapped the left leg of one to the left leg of the other, two feet of slack. Just enough for them to walk but making running difficult.

Dave did double duty by keeping a close eye on Ruben while listening for any news on the radio.

Noon came and passed. I thought for sure our EVAC chopper would of have arrived. I got on the radio. "Cameraman to North Star. Cameraman to North Star," I waited for a response. "Cameraman checking on the ETA for our ride."

An emotionless voice came over the radio. "For security verification, what is your home state?"

"Idaho 123," was my replied. Idaho 123 was my verification password. I set up before leaving. It was intended for situations where there was uncertainty about the identity of the person on the other end.

"It's good to hear from you. We were told someone had canceled your EVAC."

"Who the fuck canceled our EVAC?" I screamed into that mic.

"Your Captain told us your squad had been wiped out in a firefight."

Only one captain would even think of doing such an evil, unprofessional act. If Captain Phillips was in my reach, I would of have strangled him with no remorse and I didn't care who heard me. I turned to the squad. "Shit! Shit! I am going to kill one Captain Phillips and whoever else is responsible for leaving us out here."

I took a deep breath and keyed the mic. "No, we are still alive with one wounded and two NVA prisoners. We have been waiting for EVAC since sunrise."

"I can get two Hueys to your position in maybe one hour."

"One hour, you better hurry with those Hueys. If they delay for too long, they will just be picking up our dead bodies."

One hour and thirty minutes passed. The anger and nervousness rose to a point I had to push my emotions down until we got back to Da Nang. At any moment, I expected to see a platoon of NVA soldiers charging our position. Every one of them, ready to take payback on us.

"Snatch and Grab calling Cameraman," came over the radio.

"Cameraman here."

"Snatch here. We will be over your position in less than five. Do we have to worry about any opposition to us picking you up?"

"Unknown. We have been sitting here longer than I would like. When we hear you, we'll put out red smoke fifty feet south of our position."

"Roger, that good buddy."

The sound of two UH-D Hueys accompanied by a gunship came over the eastern tree line. I signaled Leroy to release the red smoke.

The first Huey touched down. I heard a cracking sound from an AK-47. I turned my head to see several muzzles flashing. We went from an easy EVAC to dodging bullets while getting on the Hueys.

The NVA commander played it smart. Instead of over running our position and killing us, he waited. By waiting he could take us out and at least one EVAC chopper.

Pham and I watched as the first Huey loaded and headed back to base. As soon as the first one took off and the second one touched down. I fired my rifle toward the muzzle flashes until my ammo clip was empty. Out of ammo, I headed toward the second Huey. Everyone was inside except Pham. I saw him running toward the Huey.

Two NVA came running at me. Taking my Browning HP, I fired at them. I waited until I saw Pham board the chopper, then I ran in that direction. All I remember was falling on my face. My side screamed in pain. I opened my eyes enough to see the Huey lift off and headed east to Da Nang. My vision faded to black.

AS POW

My head hurt worse than any hangover had before or since. My ribs screamed when I took a breath.

I opened my eyes to blurry figures standing over me against a dark background. To the best of my knowledge, I had to of been out for several hours. Night had fallen. It appeared as if they were examining my condition. I tried to focus on the details of their faces. I was able to recognize the tan color of their uniforms. Opening and closing my eyes didn't make them go away.

"Wake up American soldier, Wake up!" I felt a sharp pain from a boot in my ribs. Another boot and a less sharp pain on my butt.

I opened my eyes just as if a boot landed in the middle of my stomach.

I jerked and rolled away from those standing over me. Another boot landed just above my left kidney.

A boot pushed me onto my back. It held me there. I looked up to see more faces standing around me.

The more they talked, the louder they got. They must of have been arguing about what they were to do with me. I wanted them to waste time so I could figure out where I was at and what I could do to escape.

With my eyes closed, I wanted them to think I was fading in and out of consciousness. Lieutenant Doyle once told me if your captors think you are unconscious, they will leave you alone.

A boot landed right on my hip. I tried not to flinch. Instead, I let out a grunt. One of my captors bent over me. He then stood up and proceeded to plant his boot on my face. I moved out of the way. His boot landed on the ground inches from my head.

"So, you awake, American soldier." I heard in broken English.

"What is your name?" My other captor asked.

"Rob…berts, Ja…son Rob…berts," It hurt to speak.

They must of have been kicking on me for some time, to get me conscious. It didn't matter how hard I tried; I could not find any part of my body that didn't hurt.

My vision kept going in and out of focus. The flickering light from a distant fire on my captor's faces confirmed I must of have been out for quite some time.

"What is your rank, soldier? What is your unit? I don't see any patches on your shoulders. Are you a spy?"

"Na, na, no, I'm just a combat photographer." C4 had the practice of not wearing patches of rank or unit when in the field. We just wore one patch: that of an American flag. Wearing that patch kept us from being labeled as spies.

"Where is your camera? Mister Combat Photographer?"

"First chopper took it. My sergeant did not want to lose the pictures I took."

"You lie. We know better."

"We know you help kill a lot of North Vietnamese soldiers."

"I'm just a combat photographer who takes pictures." I figured it would be best for me to keep with my story. At least part of it was true. I arrived in Vietnam as a combat photographer. I never planned on being the squad leader of a Long Range Recon Patrol.

Another boot landed in my ribs. "You lie. Tell us the truth."

"I'm telling you the truth." I blurted out in anger. "What can I do to convince you?" I needed to convincingly act the part of a combat photographer being wrongly accused. I had heard stories of the torture they would put NCOs and officers through. Playing the part of a combat photographer was my way of reducing the punishment they would inflict on me.

My two interrogators looked at each other. A third North Vietnamese soldier walked up and started yelling at the other two. Then the three walked off.

While they were gone, I took stock in my physical condition and surroundings. They tied my hands over my head. They bound my feet together. A rope went from my hands to a tree a couple of feet away.

Quite some time later, my captors came back. One gave me a drink from a dirty canteen. Then he poured the rest on my head. Another captor untied the ropes around my feet. He lifted me onto my feet. Another placed a black hood over my head.

Someone placed a looped rope around my neck and pulled on it until I choked. It pulled me forward. A second rope got looped around my neck. It got pulled tight. I felt it tug backwards. My mind drifted to the picture of a dog with two leashes, each pulling him in a different direction.

I felt the front rope jerk and heard. "Walk American Prisoner, walk."

The black hood kept me from telling which direction they were leading me.

As we walked a bit, I could sense the sun's heat on my body. Before they put the hood on me, I figured it must have been early morning. We walked with the sun at my left side. That meant they had to be leading me toward Ho Chi Minh Trail and eventually to Hotel Hanoi. Everything I had heard about Hotel Hanoi made it the last place I wanted to visit.

I figured we had to be somewhere along the 16th parallel. If they were taking me westward from where they captured me, we would reach the Laotian border in the next day or two. After that, I could give up all hope of getting home when my enlistment was up.

ON THE MOVE

I tried to play it cool, acting like a dumb combat photographer. I wanted my captors to relax their guard around me. Now I started forming a plan to escape. I knew for my escape plan to work they had to believe my story and not see me as a threat. It seemed to work.

My captors laughed more and more. From the way they would shoot glances in my direction, I could tell they were making jokes about me. The United States Army taking off and leaving a combat photographer behind. They must of have joked among themselves that I was a terrible photographer.

"Mister Combat Photographer," They repeatedly asked me. "What did you do that made them want to leave you behind?"

Acting like an innocent victim, I would say, "I don't know. They took my camera, gave me a gun. They told me to shoot you guys. The next thing I knew, the chopper took off, leaving me behind."

"I am told you killed a couple of my men."

"I'm sorry. They were running at me. I wanted to stop them."

"What about my supply convoy? Were you there?"

"I just took pictures."

"Where were you when your soldiers killed my men?"

"Behind the radioman. They got mad at me. I stepped on a dry branch. It snapped. Then everyone started shooting. After it was over, I took the pictures."

I felt a boot landed in the joint behind my knees. "You lie."

My knees buckled. The next thing I saw was dirt and leaves. I had to keep up my story regardless of how they treated me. I spat dirt out of my mouth as they pulled me to my feet.

After a few more pointed questions, I came back like I was getting angry. "Can't you get it? I know very little! How many times do I have to tell you? I'm just a photographer. I'm not a soldier!"

Finally, I think they gave up. The hood got put back over my head. Without warning, one of the ropes around my neck jerked downward. It kept pulling until I was on my hands and knees.

They untied my hands from behind me. They slammed my face against this tree. While facing the tree, they wrapped my arms and legs around it. My hands and feet tied together on the other side of the tree.

I liked the idea of resting at night, but I didn't like the position they put me in. All I knew was I had to come up with a way to escape. The longer I waited, the more I would be further into enemy territory and less the chances of making it to a friendly village.

I flashed back to some of what the instructor said in the Escape and Evasion class. Funny thing, I remember the class, but the only thing I remember was him saying, "Never give up. Always look for a way to escape."

The longer I stayed a prisoner, the weaker I would get. My captors only gave me a sip or two of water when they felt like it. Their idea of dinner comprised some slop with rice in it. It didn't have any flavor.

I shifted my weight and position to something less painful.

When my muscles cramping got unbearable, I had to shift my position again. Ultimately, every position caused cramps and pain.

In pain and hopelessly hugging a tree, my mind searched for some pleasant mental picture where I could draw hope. I had to hold out. All I wanted to do was go back home and have Thanksgiving dinner with my parents. Then the image popped into my mind. I shut my eyes to see Lieutenant Alice Doyle. She appeared sitting beside a pool in a red bikini. She got up and walked toward me with a smile.

The same smile I saw while on our way to get Sergeant Psycho's body. The smile she had while handing me a peanut butter and jelly sandwich. She made the point she not only fixed my favorite peanut butter and jelly sandwich, but she fixed it the way I like it.

I opened my eyes, expecting to see her. All I saw was the inside of that black hood. I closed my eyes one more time. I tried to imagine spending time with Alice Doyle out of uniform.

HOPE BECOMES REAL

The cool morning dew provided a pleasant relief from the cramping pain I endured. I found by moving my head around a few times, I could position the hood so I could see out from under it.

If I heard my captors coming in my direction, I would twist my head a little to the right. My hood fell back into place. Hearing the birds singing their morning song in the distance relaxed me. My ears caught the sound of the rippling water from a stream.

I pictured getting out of my ropes and escaping. A cool, refreshing drink from the stream would be nice. I could follow the stream through the jungle until I came upon a river. There had to be a friendly village downstream of that river. Maybe the stream could lead me to a group of American soldiers on patrol. I felt confident if I could get free from these ropes; I could find my way back to Da Nang.

I twisted and pulled on my ropes, hoping to work free. They only got tighter. I wanted to have the strength of Superman, so I could pull and break free and reunite with C4. The idea of spending time in Hanoi became more real with each passing hour.

My nose caught the smell of burning wood from a campfire. These NVA soldiers were drinking coffee instead of tea, like I had heard. I so wish they would offer me a cup. Sergeant Psycho never let us have a campfire to make morning coffee when on a mission.

I figured the Ho Chi Minh Trail would be another day's walk. From there, I would get loaded on the back of some truck headed north.

A familiar sound grew louder. It came closer and closer. I recognized the sound of chopper blades slicing through the air. They got louder. Could it be I was getting rescued? My heart pounded with excitement. I pushed back my weakness. I wanted to be able to travel when I got rescued.

Just as quickly as the sound of chopper blades got louder, the sound faded off into the distance. My heart sank in despair. I didn't want to be a prisoner of war. I felt like I had lost my fight.

In my head, I heard Lieutenant Doyle's voice, "Slow down. Breathe slowly." I needed to put into practice her words. I took in five deep breaths. After each, I exhaled, gradually.

Pop! Pop! Pop! My whole body jumped, not expecting to hear the sound of gunfire. No way. I recognized the sound of those semiautomatic weapons. I heard voices screaming in panic. Other voices shouting orders in English. I tried to move my hood to glimpse as to the events happening around me. I could not.

The voice of one of my captors said something in Vietnamese. Then I heard two more pops. I thought I heard him scream in pain. Another loud pop resonated close to me.

Some of the popping sounds came from AKs. Most of the semi auto fire came from the CAR-15s. Yes, those popping sounds were coming from a CAR-15. MAC V operatives and C4 were the only ones I knew had them.

My arms fell limp. My ropes no longer pulled around the tree. I fell backwards. Two sets of arms reach undermine and pull me to my wobbly legs. I had trouble standing. The hood lifted off my head.

I blinked my eyes twice to focus on my surroundings. There, standing around me, were Mick, Dave, Leroy, Sparky, and Pham.

"Can you walk?" Dave asked.

I shifted my weight from one leg to the next. "I'll give it my best."

"We will help you," Dave said. "We got to get you to a safe place. No telling who is going to show up on this trail." Dave put his arm around my waist and helped me walk.

The squad led me off into the jungle for about an hour or more. We stopped for a quick rest. Dave opened and gave me a can of peaches.

"Here, eat these. They will give you some strength," Dave said.

"Thank you. Thank you." I have never been so grateful in all my life.

"We couldn't leave you out here. What would we do without our sergeant?" Mick said.

"How did you get permission to come back after me?" I asked. "I thought I had got a one way ticket to the Hanoi Hilton."

Mick leaned forward and looked me in the eye. "We couldn't leave you behind. We didn't want to break in another squad leader."

"How did you find me?"

Leroy smiled. "A pilot from the 219th Aviation Company spotted a group of NVA leading a prisoner west. We knew it had to be you."

Mick picked up the narrative. "Our beloved captain refused to launch a rescue mission for you."

"I'm not surprised."

Sparky added. "He said since you were dumb enough to get caught, you deserve the treatment they give you."

"How did you get permission to come and rescue me?"

"We didn't. We bribed a Huey and gunship crew with a couple cases of Hamm's beer each."

"Where did you get that much Hamm's?"

A grin rose on everyone's face. They looked like a group of cats that had just eaten a pet shop full of canaries.

"Did you get them from Lieutenant Doyle?" I asked. I figured only the Lieutenant would have the resources to get that much beer on such short notice.

They nodded. I smiled.

"Are we headed back for a court martial?" I asked.

"We got a better plan. I think you are going to like it," Mick said.

WHAT'S NEXT

"Hey, Dave," I asked. "How bad was Ruben's wound?"

"His wound wasn't that bad. But when we got to Da Nang, he jumped out of the Huey and broke his leg."

"How did he manage that?"

"It's my fault. While on the way back, I may of have given him a little too much morphine. So, when we got to Da Nang, Ruben was the first to jump out of the Huey. The Huey was six feet from the ground. He broke his leg in a couple of places."

"Is Ruben going to be alright?"

"They are shipping him to Okinawa for more x-rays and recovery. We might see him later. It all depends upon what happens to us."

I looked at Mick. "So, what is the plan for being better than a court-martial?"

"We don't." When Mick spoke those words, my heart sank. I understood the severity of the situation when the guy's defied direct orders, but without an exit plan, we would be classified as deserters, risking imprisonment when apprehended.

"Mick, you said you had a plan. Now you say you don't have a plan. What gives?"

"Colonel Beck and Lieutenant Doyle came up with this plan. We just have to execute it. At the same time, we get to payback Captain Phillips for leaving us out here and trying to get us all killed. In addition, you get to do some payback on General Moorehead."

"What does Colonel Beck and Lieutenant Doyle want in exchange?"

"This is the best part. We get to perform a covert mission that will prove to the United States Military what we can do and what needs to be done to win this war."

"How is that?" I asked.

Pham handed me my camera case. I opened it to see my camera and several rolls of film. Seeing it, I had to smile. "I take it we are not headed back to Da Nang."

"Lieutenant Doyle wanted you to have your camera. She has arranged for the photos you took of Captain Phillips barbecues placed in the bottom of your camera case. All we have to do is get you and your pictures to the American Embassy in Saigon. They will forward the photos to the Pentagon."

"What is the camera and rolls of film for?"

"That is the fun part. We are to go to Saigon via the Ho Chi Minh Trail. You are to take pictures of any North Vietnamese troop movements we come across and document any destruction of supply flowing the Ho Chi Minh Trail. Lieutenant Doyle will be waiting for us at Quan Loi. From there, we will have an escort to Saigon."

"Colonel Beck and Lieutenant Doyle are crazy." Came the words out of my mouth when I heard the plan. I almost wanted to get recaptured by the NVA soldiers. "That's a suicide mission. What makes any of you think we can pull it off?"

I closed my eyes for a moment and took a deep breath. I waited for their answer. When it didn't come, I took another breath and calmly stated my objections. "That is close to two hundred to three hundred miles on foot. If we could travel twenty miles a day. It would take us close to fifteen days or more. We would be exhausted. Not to mention any NVA or Viet Cong we would come across would slow us down. What are we going to do for ammo?"

Sparky answered, "Remember what Lieutenant Doyle suggested one time? When we run out of ammo, we take weapons and ammo off those we kill. Besides, when we are ready to head out, we are getting some supplies."

Mick continued filling me in on the plan details. "I picture this mission would be a get even or die mission. We are to head south of our current position. At a special place, there is a cave with some supplies. It is a good place for us to rest up. From there, we are to load up with what we can carry and travel on the Ho Chi Minh Trail. At the same time, creating confusion and destruction."

Dave offered me a way out. "If you are not up for this mission, me and the rest of C4 will do it."

"No way!" This was one mission I definitely wanted to be in on. I wanted to see Captain Phillips and General Moorehead's faces when confronted with their hypocrisy. The evidence will get them a court marshaled. The idea of seeing them sent to prison put a smile on my face.

TIME TO REST UP

Mick filled me in with more details as he knew them. "A few clicks south of here is a cave. The special forces operatives use the cave to stash supplies for when they are in the area."

"What if they come by when we are there, won't they take us back as deserters?" I asked.

"It is my understanding they have been told a special classified mission is using their cave as a launch point. They are to stay clear until told otherwise."

Sparky added. "I don't understand how Colonel Beck arranged it, but we are now a classified unit on a classified mission. We are to have access to any reports of spotted NVA movement in our direction."

Mick went back to filling me in on the details. "Lieutenant Doyle gave us a special radio frequency to contact them when we are ready to head out, and another frequency for when we are close to our extraction point."

I had always suspected Colonel Beck had more juice than some Generals. Sometime later, I found out Colonel Beck oversaw all the CIA operations in South Vietnam, including Laos and Cambodia. I often wanted to know who his boss was besides the President of the United States

While at the cave, we spent most of the time sitting around eating MRE meals and cleaning our weapons. Still, we were in a war zone. The enemy could come upon us at any time. We couldn't fire our weapons unless we would alert any NVA in the area. After three days, I felt stronger and ready to get our classified mission started. I could tell the members of the squad were getting eager to kick some butt.

On the fourth morning, I reached for the radio and turned to the special frequency. I keyed the mic. "This is Psych Ward getting ready to move out."

After I confirmed with the usual verification code, a familiar female voice came over the radio. "Santa will arrive in two hours with your Christmas presents. Hold tight until after delivery."

Leroy must of seen the bewildered look on my face. He jogged my memory as to the date. "Hey, man, don't you keep track of the holidays anymore?" I searched my mind but could think of the date. "Tomorrow is Christmas day."

I had to stop. The only thing I could say was, "I've been too busy trying to stay alive."

"I wonder what kind of Christmas present we are getting?" Dave asked.

"It better not be fruitcake," Leroy said. "I'm sick of having fruit cake. All my relatives like to send me fruit cake every year."

We waited. Our imagination ran wild, trying to figure out what kind of Christmas presents we would be getting. They could only be something that would help in our mission or eat.

Two hours to the minute later, a Huey escorted by two gunships touched down on the hill above the cave. Out the side door, we saw four wooden crates pushed out of the Huey.

Lieutenant Doyle stepped out on one of the crates, then on to the ground. She had on a red jacket with white around the collar and cuffs. On her head was a Santa hat. She ran toward me.

We stopped two feet from each other. I mustered everything in my power not to hug her. "What are you doing here?"

"I came to check up on you and bring you a few presents."

"What did you bring us?" Leroy asked, coming up beside me.

Looking me over, Lieutenant Doyle said, "I wanted to see if you are up to the little hike we arranged for you and the guys." Turning to Leroy, "I brought you some food and ammo for the trip."

"It is my understanding we are to meet you and Colonel Beck in Quin Loi in fourteen days?"

"No, Jason, eleven days. You have spent three days of the fourteen days here."

"Okay, no pressure. Eleven days to Quan Loi. How are we to do it?" Our difficult mission turned into one that would be nearly impossible. We would need some incredible luck.

Alice Doyle moved closer to me. She whispered in my ear. "I know you will find a way. I will see you there, waiting for you. You take care of yourself." She put her lips on my cheek and landed a quick kiss. Then she turned around and ran toward the Huey and jumped inside. That one kiss motivated me more than anything else for that entire mission.

The Huey lifted off the ground, taking her away.

PREPARATION TIME

The crates Doyle brought contained ammo, MREs, and an interesting selection of explosives for Sparky. Alice Doyle left me with a kiss and a map marking out our travel route. I estimated the trip to be approximately two hundred and fifty miles. All of it on foot.

The unknown factor was the Viet Cong or North Vietnamese Army traveling along the same route we would be traveling. I knew a small group of American soldiers traveling on the Ho Chi Minh Trail would give us the advantage of surprise. In December of 1968, American soldiers were not allowed to operate along the Ho Chi Minh Trail. Especially on the portion of the trail that snaked into the Cambodia side of the border.

As hopeless as it sounded to a sane person, I knew they gave us the mission because Colonel Beck and Lieutenant Doyle believed we could accomplish what needed accomplished. All the members of C4 believed we could. Regardless of my doubts, I knew their attitudes would motivate me. But the idea of getting back at General Moorehead and Captain Phillips motivated us all the more.

The Ho Chi Minh Trail had some paved spots. A large

portion of the trail consisting of uneven compacted dirt. In a few places were dried-up riverbeds. Some water crossings could of been classified as small flowing rivers. During our entire trip, I don't remember seeing a bridge.

In the four crates Lieutenant Doyle left was more than enough for our trip. The first crate consisted of enough rations for all of us for three days. The second, third, and fourth crates had unique markings on the outside. They were all labeled medical supplies.

If I saw those markings a year ago, I would have thought we were going to be providing medical assistance to some village. I had learned differently, Lieutenant Doyle liked to mislabel the important stuff. It was her way of getting restricted supplies to us without the brass looking too close as to what was inside. This time was no different.

We opened the second crate to find six new CAR-15s. The third crate contained more ammo than we could carry. We had to test fire a couple of rounds. The quality of the ammo gave us exceptional accuracy. She must have gotten it from the Mac V group.

In the last crate contained special gifts for Sparky. Plastic explosives, with electric and non-electric detonators. Sparky's eyes lit up like a kid on Christmas morning. It was Christmas morning.

Besides all the toys we received, our one big advantage came down to surprise. The Viet Cong and North Vietnamese soldiers would not be expecting a well-armed, well rested American soldiers with nothing to lose out to destroy any enemy they came across. We didn't give a rat's ass if we were in South Vietnam or Cambodia. We were headed for Saigon to take down a corrupt General and Captain who wanted to see us dead.

The rest of that day, we spent preparing a master plan. It consisted of three main parts. In the mornings we were to set up traps with explosives and punji sticks in covered holes. In the afternoon and evening, we would travel until it got too dark for us to travel.

The third part varied depending upon what we came across. If came across a caravan or a used camp site, I would take pictures before C4 went to work destroying it. After we laid it waste, I would snap another set of photographs.

We would spend the nights at least a hundred yards off the trail. We would take turns on the watch while the rest was sleeping. Leroy asked if he still could do the tree lookout. I smiled and said he could.

We spent the rest of the day packing up everything we could carry. What we couldn't carry with us, we placed in the cave for whoever needed it.

WAR WAGON

We had nine days to travel two hundred and fifty miles on foot. Back home, even with the county roads, two hundred and fifty miles would have been a problem. However, the major supply route like the Ho Chi Minh Trail did not have the luxury of a consistently smooth surface to travel. If we traveled on foot, twenty-five miles in a day, that meant it would take us ten days. I knew the odds were against us. Everyone in the squad had determined to make it to Quan Lo and on to Saigon, on schedule.

The sun had been up for several hours. Our optimism turned to discouragement quick because the reality of the physical exhaustion from hiking over twenty-five miles hit. Regardless of how we felt, we had to keep going.

About mile fifteen on the first day, I could tell the guys felt like we had bitten off more than we could chew. Then Pham tapped me on my shoulder. I turned to where he was pointing behind us.

I could see the look of excitement on his face. "Trucks! Trucks! Trucks coming! Trucks coming from the north!"

Before I could motion to take cover, every member of C4 ran

for cover on the west side of the trail. We narrowly had enough time to get into position before the trucks came upon us.

Sparky announced, "I'll slow them down, boss." He already had two grenades in his hands.

The first truck approached Sparky's position. He tossed the first grenade under the first truck. It landed right where he wanted it to land. Boom! The truck bounced up. When it came down, the truck laid on its side.

Sparky threw the second grenade in front of the second truck. Boom! The truck bounced up and stopped.

The third truck slid to a halt. I could see the driver's eyes widen in surprise. He froze. His passenger jumped out and pointed his AK in our direction. Mick landed a round between his eyes.

Pham and Dave took out the other two drivers with well-placed rounds. Those riding shotgun just set in their seats stunned. From the back of the first two trucks, several NVA soldiers staggered out, only to be met with rounds from Sparky, Mick and me.

We killed off all the drivers and riders, then we went to work inspecting the back of the trucks. The second and third truck carried bags of rice along with ammo for some Viet Cong platoon. In the back of the first truck, we found mortar rounds and other explosives.

"Hey, Sarge," Dave said. "Can we use that third truck to take us south? That way, we can definitely make it to Saigon on time."

"That is why I didn't grenade it," Sparky added.

"Great job, Sparky." I had to shoot Sparky a compliment. C4 went to work without me saying another word. Everyone knew what needed to be done and did it.

Mick supervised the loading of the third truck. He made sure there was ample space in the back for Sparky, Dave, Leroy, and himself. I had Pham drive while I rode shotgun.

Before we left, Sparky booby trapped the first two trucks and the bodies. Pham took one of their uniforms off a dead body and put on the shirt. It would confuse any Viet Cong we would come across.

In less than an hour, we were bouncing along the Ho Chi Minh Trail at the top speed. Top speed in the truck meant twenty-five miles per hour. Any faster, we could have the guys in the back getting thrown out.

We stayed on the main resupply artery to South Vietnam. The road had more potholes and ruts than one could count. Even at twenty-five miles per hour, the guys complained of being bounced around. Reluctantly, I had Pham slow down.

Having Pham drive would make any VC we ran across that we were just another supply truck. Well, until we got close enough to see me riding shotgun. By then, I planned on giving them an unpleasant surprise.

Riding in that truck bouncing around reminded me of the last movie I saw before going to Vietnam. John Wayne and Kirk Douglas starred in a movie titled War Wagon. I never dreamed I could be a modern-day John Wayne riding in my own version of the War Wagon. We were on our way to Saigon to expose a corrupt General Moorehead and Captain Phillips.

Our War Wagon happened to be a dirty gray Mercedes flatbed truck. The back was open with two six-inch sideboards. We covered the supplies with a canvas tarp.

WIPE OUT

On the morning of day eight, our contact with the enemy had been minimal. I checked the map for our location. We were undoubtedly inside Cambodia. Back then, American troops were not officially allowed to operate inside the Cambodian border. We weren't supposed to be in Laos either. However, that was where we were when we took out those three trucks.

Regardless of our successes, I still worried what if Colonel Beck's and Lieutenant Doyle's plans went south? That meant they could charge all of us as war criminals.

I could not worry about what would happen after getting to Saigon. I had to stay focused on the present. The guys in the back of the truck kept watch for any patrol catching up to us. Pham and I keep watch for coming upon any trucks or enemy personnel heading north. I wanted us to be seen as a lone supply truck heading south. I didn't want to alert any enemy patrols until we were jumping out and firing at them.

We were all feeling pretty confident when I awoke from daydreaming from the voice of Pham screaming, "Hang on! We're going to hit …!"

I felt the truck lunge forward. At the same time, a couple of the guys in the back bounced off the back of the truck's cab. Any warning to the guys in the back was too late.

Pham had put the gas pedal to the floor. We felt a quick jerk forward. Over the truck's hood, I saw bicycles, packages, and bodies flying in all different directions. The truck bounced and lunged a couple more times. We ran over what didn't get pushed out of the way.

The truck came to a stop with the rear wheels spinning. Pham pushed a pile of bodies, packages, and bicycles jammed underneath the truck, causing it to come to a stop and unable to move any further.

The squad grabbed their weapons and jumped out. They moved forward, firing at anyone that moved.

The poor VC had been pushing their bikes loaded with supplies. Pham didn't give them a chance to react to the sound or sight of our War Wagon barreling down on them. One minute, they were pushing their bikes loaded with boxes and crates. The next minute, they were getting run over by our crazy Vietnamese interpreter.

Dave came over to check on us. Pham sat with his hands gripping the wheel, smiling. Both of my hands were firmly braced against the dashboard. I sat there in a daze, staring at the carnage Pham had created. Dave came up to me. "Are you alright sarge?"

"I think so." I had pushed myself away from the windshield. My forehead left a spider like crack from the sudden stop.

"What about Pham?" I asked.

"He's not moving, but I see him breathing. I think he will need a break from driving after we clean up this mess." Dave gave Pham a quick inspection. "He's just stunned."

Shaking off the shock, I climbed out of the truck. Mick

walked around to me. "We got them all. Well, the ones Pham didn't take out. They didn't have time to fire one shot."

"Good work. Did any of the guys get hurt from Pham bulldozer job?"

"Nay, just shaken up."

"Before you go through their stuff, let me get my camera out. I want to take a few pictures. Once I'm finished, you can go through their stuff. Take whatever you think we can use and load it in the truck."

"Is the truck still drivable?" Mick asked.

"We'll have to check that out," I said. "Why don't you check it out for Pham and take over driving? Give him a break."

"Leroy, Sparky, and me will put the bikes and supplies into the drainage ditch," said Mick.

"Hey, Sparky,"

"Yo, sarge,"

"Wait until everyone finishes going through what is on the bikes. Then how about putting together some of your little surprises? If anyone comes behind us, I want their day ruined."

"It will be my pleasure, sarge."

C4 worked fast to clear the road for our War Wagon. We laid out the bikes, supplies we didn't take, and the bodies in a row. Sparky put his surprise on only two of the bikes and three of the bodies.

It took Pham and Mick a couple of hours to make the truck drivable again. Leroy found a tree to use as a lookout. Dave and I walked ahead about fifty yards to spot anyone traveling north.

It wasn't long before we were back bouncing along the Ho Chi Minh Trail in our War Wagon. We just did a hit and run. Leaving behind a couple of surprises under the bodies and packages for those who show up to clean up our mess.

I gave Pham the rest of the day to rest up. Mick took over

driving duties. I figured one crazy attack a day was enough for all of us.

We moved along at a surprisingly quick pace. Considering the amount of brush on either side of the road, I told the guys in the back to keep an eye out for any VC. I didn't want us to get ambushed, since we were deep into enemy territory, our only real advantage was surprise. We had a great advantage; I didn't want us to lose it.

The next day, we made twenty-five easy miles. We were well on our way of making it a lot more than the truck began a jerking back and forth. A coughing sound came from the engine. Our War Wagon rolled to a stop.

"What's happening?" I asked Pham.

Pham looked down at the gas gauge and back up at me. "Out of gas."

"Oh shit," were the first words that came out of my mouth. Everything was going so great, the idea of needing gas escaped me. I had been more concerned about having enough food and ammunition than fuel.

"Okay guys, get what you can carry. Leroy and Mick take point. Find us a campsite for the night. Make it about a hundred yards off the trail."

"Afterwards, shall I set up a sniper platform?" Leroy asked. "I see the perfect tree."

"Go ahead, not too high up. You may have to jump down if we have to move quickly."

"Shall do sarge."

"Sparky, you take Pham and set up some of your surprises around the truck."

"You got it sarge, come on Pham."

We were just getting settled when we heard a truck heading north. We left our abandoned truck blocking the trail. I motioned for everyone to get into position. "Be ready. We just might of have got lucky, again."

I looked around. "Where is Pham?"

Sparky motioned toward the road.

I signaled for him to get out of the truck, but Sparky said, "It's okay. Just wait and see."

The truck heading north stopped about forty feet from our abandoned War Wagon and Pham. The truck's driver and his shotgun rider climbed out of the cab. Their AK's pointing upward. They slowly walked toward ours. I could tell coming across abandon trucks was not normal. I motioned to C4 to wait until we saw what they were going to do. Another one of them climbed out of the back of their truck.

One of them opened the driver's side door to our War Wagon. I heard a pop. He fell to the ground. Pham was hiding under the dashboard of the War Wagon. When the driver opened the door Pham shot him.

Mick took out his buddy. From his tree perch, Leroy took out the third one.

When we inspected the truck, we found it empty except for two full cans of gas, plus what was in the truck's tank. We filled the tank of our War Wagon. We even had extra gas.

Most convoys didn't travel at night. If they did, it meant they would have to use their headlights. Headlights could make them easy targets.

The next morning, Pham was back driving. I made him promise to give us a little more warning before plowing into any bikes or enemy. He just smiled.

We placed the bodies of two from the north bound truck next to the road. Sparky placed a grenade under one of them. He then rigged their truck to explode when either door was opened.

We were off again, bouncing along the Ho Chi Minh Trail.

GETTING LUCKY

The next day, we made over twenty-five miles. We were well on our way of making it a lot more than the truck began a jerking back and forth. A coughing sound came from the engine. Our War Wagon rolled to a stop.

I looked at Pham. "What's happening?"

Pham looked down at the gas gauge and back up at me. "We out of gas."

"Oh shit," were the first words that came out of my mouth. Everything was going so great, the idea of needing gas escaped me. I had been more concerned about having enough food and ammunition than fuel.

"Okay guys, get what you can carry. Leroy and Mick take point. Find us at a campsite for the night. Make it about a hundred yards off the trail."

"Afterwards, shall I set up a sniper platform?" Leroy asked. "I see the perfect tree."

"Go ahead, not too high up. You may have to jump down if we get need to move."

"Shall do sarge."

"Sparky, you take Pham and set up some of your surprises around the truck."

"You got it sarge, come on Pham."

We were just getting settled when we heard a truck heading north. We left our abandoned truck blocking the trail. I motioned for everyone to get into position. "Be ready. We just might of have got lucky, again."

I looked around. "Where is Pham?"

Sparky motioned toward the road.

I signaled for him to get out of the truck, but Sparky said, "It's okay. Just wait and see."

The truck heading north stopped about forty feet from our abandoned war wagon and Pham. The truck's driver and his shotgun rider climbed out of the cab. Their AK's pointing upward. They slowly walked toward ours. I could tell coming across abandon trucks was not normal. I motioned to C4 to wait until we saw what they were going to do. Another one of them climbed out of the back of their truck.

One of them opened the driver's side door to our war wagon. I heard a pop. He flew backwards. Pham was hiding under the dashboard of the war wagon. When the driver open the door Pham shot him.

Mick took out his buddy. From his tree perch, Leroy took out the third one.

When we inspected the truck, we found it empty except for two full cans of gas, plus what was in the truck's tank. We filled the tank of the war wagon. We even had an extra full can of gas.

Most convoys didn't travel at night. If they did, it meant they would have to use their headlights. Headlights could make them easy targets.

The next morning, Pham was back driving the war wagon. I made him promise to give us a little more warning before plowing into any bikes for trucks. He just smiled.

We placed the bodies of two from the north bound truck next to the road. Sparky placed a grenade under one of them. He then rigged their truck to explode when either door was opened.

We were off again, bouncing along the Ho Chi Minh Trail in our War Wagon.

NERVOUS REST

The Ho Chi Minh Trail extended from North Vietnam all the way into South Vietnam. While winding through parts of Cambodia. At key places, the trail would branch to key supply locations in South Vietnam. Some of those branches appeared to be nothing more than a footpath.

We were given directions to take this one branch eastward to Quan Loi. Note, I said directions, not orders. We had no written orders for what we were doing. In fact, American soldiers were not supposed to be operating along the Cambodia side of the Ho Chi Minh Trail. We never understood why the politicians in Washington wanted to tie our hands the way they did.

I understood Mick and some of the squad members had talked with Colonel Beck and Lieutenant Doyle in Da Nang. I only met with Lieutenant Doyle when she gave me a map and directions. We were to meet them at Quan Loi in a certain number of days.

From what Mick and the others had told me, I can only assume that Charlie Company Fourth Squad had the status of AWOL (Absent Without Leave). I could not see Captain Phillip having classified C4 other than MIA (Missing In Action), presumed dead. Our only hope was for Colonel Beck to have the authority to make the changes to our status.

Mick and the rest of C4 said if we went back to Da Nang, C4 and me would be placed in the stockade. The entire squad had disobeyed a direct order to by rescuing me from the North Vietnamese patrol. I am sure after a very short court martial, Captain Phillips, and General Moorehead would ship us off to Leavenworth for the rest of our lives.

Our only hope for not going to jail and getting out of Vietnam alive rested on following the plan from Colonel Beck and Lieutenant Alice Doyle had outlined for us. My experience with those two told me they had major influence with the Pentagon and CIA. It wasn't until years later, after we left Vietnam, I got a clearer picture as to what those two really did.

As we approached Quan Loi, I thought more about how they could help us. All I know what they did for us was quite impressive.

After ten days, we crossed over from Cambodia and into South Vietnam. At that point, we parked the truck sideways, blocking one branch of the Ho Chi Minh Trail. Sparky set a little surprise for anyone who tried to move it. We went the rest of the way on foot to Quan Loi.

Later that day, we came across four straw wooden huts. They were built off to the right of the path we took. All our time in Nam we learned to expect empty building to be rigged with explosives or other kind of traps. Sparky went to check out each hut. He found nothing that would cause us harm. A rest stop before heading to Quan Loi; I thought.

Inside one hut were MREs and fresh drinking water, along with clean uniforms. In a corner, a walkie talkie. Attached to it, a note that read, "Call when you are ready to come in."

The other three huts had two cots each. On each cot a clean set of Army greens. Beside them were more water and soap.

"Do you think this stuff is meant for us, sarge?" Mick asked, giving me a look that it could be too good to be true. Inside, I agreed with him.

"This is creepy," said Leroy. "It is like they set everything out for us."

"Who else would be coming in from the Trail?" Dave asked.

"You're right, Dave. Let's rest up and I will make the call in the morning." I said.

We rotated keeping watch and throughout the night. Those of us who were not on guard duty tried to sleep with one eye open. Our weapons stayed right beside us.

The night passed very uneventfully. The morning came, we ate breakfast, and got ready to move out.

I pressed the button on the walkie talkie. "This is Cameraman calling for Pickup."

"What is your verification?" came a voice from the other end.

"Idaho 123." Nobody informed me about any changes to my verification code.

"Yes, sir, Sergeant Roberts," came a friendly voice back over the radio.

"We will be sending you transportation. It should be arriving in about an hour. A warm welcome will be here waiting for you when you get here."

I finished my roll of the film by taking pictures of the huts and the squad in clean uniforms. We moved a hundred yards back into the jungle as a precautionary measure. My stomach knotted. I was afraid of going all that distance in record time and being attacked by an ambush of Viet Cong or US Army troops.

Pham was the first to hear the sound of truck engines heading our way. I looked up to see two trucks coming our way, being led by a jeep. They were right on time. They were even coming from the direction of Quin Loi.

As they approached, I could see the faces of the drivers and those riding shotguns. Each one wore a helmet. The front of their helmet was a white field. Two black letters stood out in a white field. I squinted to make out those letters. They were M and P.

UNEXPECTED WELCOME

Both trucks and jeep stopped twenty feet from us. The driver and passenger climbed out. Two more soldiers appeared from the back of each truck. All wore helmets and arm bans displaying the black letter of MP. I knew instantly we were screwed. Colonel Beck could not of have sent the Military Police to escort us.

The leader of the group supported Master Sergeant stripes and a stone haughty look of condemnation. The other MPs supported the facial expression seen in a high stakes poker game.

"Sergeant Jason Roberts?" The Master Sergeant asked.

"That is me," I took a full step forward. I could feel C4 take a half step closer behind me.

"Is this the group known as the Charlie Company Fourth Squad?"

"Yes, it is. What is going on?"

"Under Military Code 10, Section 885, Article 85, we are placing you and these men under arrest."

"What for?"

"Our orders show you and your squad deserted their post and disobeyed direct orders. You are charged with desertion. Your men willfully disobeyed direct orders, then left their post to join the ranks of the enemy. I am also told there will be more charges to come."

Stunned, I asked about the one person I knew who could help us. "Where is Colonel Beck? We have been operating under his orders."

"We know nothing about any Colonel Beck. Our orders come directly from General Moorehead."

Another MP with sergeant stripes stepped forward. "We need all of you men to put down your weapons, turn around and get on your knees to be handcuffed."

"Where is Colonel Beck?" Mick asked, grabbing a tight hold on his rifle. "We have been operating under his direct orders."

"We don't know of any Colonel Beck. Our orders came directly from General Moorehead. We are to confiscate all your weapons and all other materials you may have with you."

I caught out of the corner of my eye all the members of C4's right foot moving back, in a battle ready posture. They were getting ready to fight and take out those MPs.

I raised my hand with my palm, pointing to them. Our hand signal to stand down. "There is no need. We don't need to make matters worse. Let us just do as they say. When we get to base, we'll get everything worked out."

"But Sarge," said Sparky. "We can take these guys with no problem."

I felt the tension mounting. The MPs were stiffing up. Their hands moved to the top of their sidearms. I had to get us out of there peacefully. "Let's just go along with them for now. We'll get this all worked out."

None of us spoke on that long, uncomfortable ride back to

Saigon. Handcuffed with our hands behind us didn't help. They put our gear in the second truck and us in the first.

We arrived at the stockade in Saigon and placed in three different cells. I had one cell to myself. In the next cell, they crowded Sparky, Mick, Leroy, and Dave. They put Pham in a cell by himself, being a Vietnamese and classified as an enemy. Pham sat in his cell staring at the floor and not saying a word.

"Sarge, what do you think will happen next?" Dave asked.

Just then, General Moorehead and Captain Phillips walked into our cell block. That blond-haired sergeant taking up the rear. Not one member of the squad bothered to snap at attention or salute. I stood up.

General Moorehead addressed the Captain. "I want to add disrespect to commanding officers to all these men's charges."

"Yes, sir," Captain Phillips said. He looked over at the sergeant, who jotted it down on the clipboard.

"Well, Sergeant Roberts, I should say soon to be just Mister Roberts. I still don't understand how you got your promotion. However, since I can't get you killed off, I am going to get you and all of your men shot for desertion and treason."

"But sir, we were under orders from Colonel Beck. If you talk to him, he will tell you we were operating under orders."

"I don't know any Colonel Beck. I heard you told the MPs the same story. There is no record of any Colonel Beck in or ever has been in Vietnam."

"We're screwed!" I thought, but I didn't say. I knew the guys next to me were thinking the same thing.

"Sir, If I remember correctly, Military Justice Code says we are entitled to have a hearing. When it that to be?" I asked.

"So, you are a lawyer now?"

"No sir, I just remembered something they told us back in boot camp. If I remember correctly, sir, disciplinary action cannot be carried out unless a hearing, and verdict, comes first."

"We had a hearing and sentence given while you were out taking your little field trip. The captain has arranged for you and your squad to be transferred to Leavenworth for execution as soon as possible."

WHERE IS OUR HELP

We were not expecting a hero's welcome, but we certainly didn't expect a prison cell and execution. Life can have its depressing twists and turns. Every member of the squad and myself wanted to see justice done and make a difference. We sat in the stockade waiting. Waiting for transportation to the states side and our execution as traitors. A long way from justice being done.

Where is Colonel Beck? Where is Lieutenant Doyle? We really needed them. We always suspected them to be spooks. They were to meet us at Quan Loi.

All the pictures I took while traveling on the Ho Chi Minh Trail are gone. My cameras gone. All the proof of what we really did, gone.

We had no malicious intent toward the United States of America. But toward General Moorehead, the general who seems to take full personal advantage of his rank. And Captain Phillips, the captain who likes to play kiss ass. Are the ones who should be sitting in these jail cells, not us.

We huddled around the bars of our jail cells so the guards would not overhear what we were discussing.

Sparky suggested. "If I could get my hands on about a half pound of plastic explosives and a couple of blasting caps. I could get us out of here in a hot second."

Mick saw the flaw in Sparky's plan. "We could get out of the stockade, but where could we go? Every American and Vietnamese soldier would be looking for us."

Dave added. "Knowing General Moorehead, he would put a bounty on our heads, 'Dead or alive; preferably dead.'"

I thought my plan was the best. "The best time for us to escape would be during transport back to the states. Once back in the states, we would have the advantage of knowing the language and the land. I even know where we could live off the grid for years."

Leroy agreed. "That sounds like the best course of action. As long as I don't end up back in Georgia. I always wondered what it would be like to live in Idaho."

Pham asked. "You guys are lucky. Do you think they are going to release me or shoot me?"

I had to reassure Pham. "You are part of this squad. We stick together. This maybe our way of getting you to the States."

"You mean, I get to go to the United States with you? But will they put me in front of a firing squad, too?"

I realized I said the wrong thing. "Pham, I meant to say we will make sure they do not put you in front of a firing squad."

The second night locked up in the stockade. I was having trouble falling asleep. My mind raced through at what point and the different ways we could escape and where we could go.

Well, after lights out that night, I got awakened by tapping on my jail cell bars. My eyes focus on the figure standing at the cell's door. Dressed in the uniform of a lieutenant stood Lieutenant Alice Doyle.

I jumped off my cot and ran toward her. "What is going on? Why has no one has ever heard of you and Colonel Beck?"

She put her figure to her lips. "Calm down. Calm down. One of the General's staff overheard your request for pick up. When the General found out, he sent the MPs before we could get there. To justify his orders, he told the MPs we did not exist."

"What about Colonel Beck can't he pull some strings to get us out of here?"

"The Colonel has got a plan to get you out. I think you are going to like the little something extra he has arranged for you."

"That is well and good, but why hasn't anyone ever heard of him or you?"

"Have you ever heard of the Central Intelligence Agency?" When Alice Doyle spoke those words, she confirmed all my unspoken suspicions.

"I take it Colonel Beck is not Army? So, what about you?"

"I will explain more later. For now, I need to tell you what is going to happen tomorrow morning."

"What is going to happen?" Standing on the wrong side of a jail made it hard for me to trust the woman I knew as Lieutenant Doyle.

"You are going to be transported states side separately from the other squad members. Tomorrow, the MPs will get orders to take you to the airfield and load you on a HH-3E Jolly Green Giant. Once inside, sit toward the very back. Cover up with the tarp lying on the seat. There will be three other passengers that will sit in front of you. When you hear the word, 'Come out, Sergeant, take the tarp off."

"Who else is going to be in that chopper?"

"Trust me. You will like what is going to happen."

HELICOPTER RIDE

The next morning, breakfast consisted of watery oatmeal, powdered eggs, and a slice of day old toast. I forced it all down. What Lieutenant Doyle did not say, made me concerned as to what would be required of me.

Just like Lieutenant Doyle said, a Military Police officer found me laying on the cot when he opened my cell door. "Get up. We have orders to take you to the airfield. You are going on a little helicopter ride."

"Where did your orders come from?" I asked.

"From General Moorehead himself."

I thought, "Oh no, the General must of have intercepted Colonel Beck's plans again."

The MP escorted me to the shower room. He handed me soap and a razor. "Get cleaned up. They want you presentable."

I finished my shower. The MP pointed to a stack of neatly folded green Army fatigues, along with underwear and socks. The boots looked like someone had taken the time to give them a spit shine.

As I finished lacing my boots, the MP was joined by another MP. They handcuffed me. Afterwards, The two of them escorted me to the Tan San Nhut airfield where a Jolly Green Giant waited.

My escort uncuffed me. "My orders are to see you get on board and leave. Get in and good luck." I climbed aboard and they drove off.

Like what Lieutenant Doyle said, I sat in the back and covered myself with a tarp.

A few minutes later, I heard three distinct voices talking. They climbed in and set ahead of where I was sitting.

I peeked out from under edge of the tarp. All I could see were their backs. All three voices sounded familiar. One was definitely Lieutenant Doyle. I heard one of the other two male voices say, "Who else will be meeting us besides the local villagers?"

"I don't know, sir. All I know is that Captain Phillips arranged the meeting. Miss Janet Young, here came along as our interpreter."

"Miss Young, after we get back, I would like to see you in my office." That voice could only be General Moorehead's. Only he would hit on a female upon meeting them.

The other male voice had to come from Colonel Beck. "It is my understanding the village leaders will grant you the usage rights of the land north of their village in exchange for protection."

"Why couldn't the Captain seal the deal himself?"

"The village leaders wanted confirmation of the deal from you directly, General."

The blades of the HH-3E increased in speed. It wasn't long before the Jolly Green Giant lifted off the ground. I could tell we were heading west. About thirty minutes into the flight, we descended and hovered.

"Oh, General, we have a little surprise for you."

"What is it?" The confident General never liked surprises.

"Sergeant, would you show yourself?"

I pulled the tarp back. I love the look on the General's face when he turned around and saw me. Yes sitting next to him were Colonel Beck and Lieutenant Doyle. They had a satisfied look on their faces.

I waved and smiled. "Hello General."

"What are you doing here?" Demanded General Moorehead.

"If I may, General, the two sitting next to you happen to be Colonel Beck of the Central Intelligence Agency. The beautiful lady sitting next to him is Lieutenant Alice C Doyle, his assistant."

The General shot a glance at both of them. He remained speechless.

The Colonel introduced himself. "I am known as Colonel Beck. I am with the Central Intelligence. Sergeant Roberts and his squad were working under my direct orders."

"Well, Colonel or whoever you are. I am a General in the United States Army. I out rank you. We are turning this helicopter around and going back to base right now."

Colonel Beck put up his hand. "General, with all due respect, you are not going back to Tan San Nhut. You have been such a disgrace to that uniform you are wearing. In addition, you have given us so much trouble we are turning you over to the North Vietnamese as punishment."

The helicopter hovered three feet above the ground as Doyle slid open the door.

Colonel Beck looked at me. "Do you want to the honors in delivering the General to those below?"

I looked out the door. Waiting below were at least a dozen black pajama-clad Vietnamese. They appeared like hungry dogs waiting for a steak.

"Are we delivering a United States General to the Viet Cong?" I asked in disbelief. "Isn't this treason?"

"If we took the General through a trial and court-marshal, it would inflict more damage to the reputation of the United States. This way the General gets punished with minimum damage to the United States."

I sat there staring at the General, thinking about all the things he said and did to me. Still, I could not push the General. Lieutenant Doyle moved to sit beside me. "Push the General out. That an order, soldier."

I looked at Colonel Beck. He said. "Do it."

"If you can't push him out of this chopper. The General will continue to get away with all his crimes." Lieutenant Doyle admonished me.

I grabbed the General by his lapel and pulled him toward me. In another swift motion, I pushed him out of the chopper. The General fell on the ground. I watched as his capturers picked him up and carried him off into the jungle.

The Jolly Green Giant regained altitude and headed back to base. I looked at Colonel Beck and over to Lieutenant Doyle. "Turning the General over to the Viet Cong. Won't the General be giving away military secrets?"

Colonel Beck smiled. "Jason, we have been feeding the General believable false information for weeks. If he makes it to Moscow alive, they will either kill him or put him in a Russian prison. I have made arrangements that he will never be part of any prisoner exchange."

HOMECOMING

The Jolly Green Giant touched down at the same place where we left an hour before. Not far away, a jeep waited with a driver for our return.

Lieutenant Doyle pointed in its direction. "Jason, the Jeep is waiting for you to join with C4."

I began to climb in the back of the Jeep, expecting Colonel Beck or Lieutenant Doyle to sit next to the driver. Instead, Colonel Beck said. "Sit up there. The driver will take you to a safe house just off base. Your squad will arrive there soon, if not there already."

I wondered what else he had planned for us.

"Tomorrow, at thirteen hundred hours, a bus will pick you and your squad up. It will take you to Tan Sun Nhut. From there, a troop transport will take you and C4 to Hawaii. After a week of R and R, all of you will be given full honorable discharges."

I looked at Lieutenant Doyle and asked. "Will I ever see you again?"

"Maybe, sometimes, or some other place maybe."

Several years ago, a reporter asked me about my experience in Vietnam. I told him essentially the same thing you have read in the previous pages. Afterward, he gave me a look of disbelief. He asked, "I don't remember any American General being captured by the Viet Cong?"

I responded by saying, "There wasn't one officially. If you remember, there was a rumor about the Viet Cong kidnapping some high-ranking Army officer. That high-ranking Army officer ended up in North Vietnam and later taken to Moscow.

"So, you're telling me that a General of the United States Army who you pushed out of a helicopter to be turned over to the North Vietnamese just to get rid of him?"
"No, what I just told you was a story from an old man who spent some time in Vietnam as a combat photographer. I am not saying the story I told you is true."

"What about Colonel Beck, Captain Phillips, and Lieutenant Doyle?"

I cracked a smile out of the corner of my mouth. "That's a story of another day. Thank you for allowing me to take up your time." I stood up and escorted the reporter out of my cabin.

The End For Now

ACKNOWLEDGMENTS

Thank you Norma and Arden Cussins for putting up with me, and my constant telling of the story and its progress.

Thank you to those who helped edit, Storytellers Critique Group, my beta readers, and Paula my editor, who pointed out things that needed fixing.

When I wrote this book, I wanted to express my gratitude to those who endured wading through the rice paddies and cut their way through the thick jungles. I didn't want to forget those who flew overhead, helped the wounded, and worked to ensure no one got left behind in South Vietnam.

ABOUT EF CUSSINS

EF has stood on top of a breeder reactor and been in the bowels of a submarine. He has seen life begin and watch life fade.

In his life, he has done wrong and done good. History will unquestionably remember the wrong he has done.

Since EF can't change the past, he is working to change his future. Part of that is to share his observations and stories.

The goal is to uplift and challenge his readers' thoughts and perceptions. Perceptions lead to making us better than who we currently are.

Find EF at EFWrites.com

9 798990 753204